Sun of a Beach

A Novella

MIA SOSA

Sun of a Beach

Copyright © 2023 by Mia Sosa

Ebook ISBN: 9781641972598

KDP POD ISBN: 9798392672462

IS POD ISBN: 9781641972666

Cover illustration by Kim Ekdahl

Cover design by VMC Art & Design

NYLA Publishing

121 W 27th St., Suite 1201, New York, NY 10001

https://www.nyliterary.com

PRAISE FOR MIA SOSA

"Sosa brilliantly plays to all of her literary strengths as she effectively channels the electric sexual chemistry between her opposites-attract protagonists into a gorgeously romantic and gloriously sensual love story that is then further enriched with a generous measure of the author's saucy sense of wit."
— Booklist (starred review)

"*The Wedding Crasher* is a winner—thoroughly delightful, modern and fun… It's laugh-out-loud funny, tartly sweet and scorching hot—a delicate balance that only a writer of Sosa's considerable talent can strike."
— BookPage (starred review)

"Mia Sosa is among the elite authors writing truly laugh-out-loud funny romantic comedies. . . the chemistry between Solange and Dean and the twisty plot are sure to delight."
— Book Riot

"Mia Sosa serves up a steamy, laugh-out-loud romance [with] *The Wedding Crasher*. The large Afro-Brazilian family the author has created is so warm, funny and nosy that readers will want to spend more time with them. Solange and Dean's banter alone is enough to recommend the novel, but Sosa manages to fill the prose with everything romance fans could want: food, family, heat and humor."
— Shelf Awareness

"*The Wedding Crasher* is a frothy, hilarious, steamy rom-com with poignant moments of vulnerability that reaffirms Mia's masterful ability to deliver genuine humor in deeply romantic stories brimming with Afro-Brazilian culture."
— Adriana Herrera for Entertainment Weekly

Praise for *The Worst Best Man*

"*The Worst Best Man* is rom-com perfection . . . . Sosa has a gift with words that's infectious and wry, one that keeps the pages turning in delight."
— Entertainment Weekly

"Bursting with humor and drama, this enemies-to-lovers rom-com is worthy of a Hollywood treatment."
— Apple Books (a Best Books of the Month selection)

"A delightful read that is equal parts sexy, heartwarming, and seriously funny."
— Elizabeth Acevedo, National Book Award Winner

"The plot is classic 'enemies to lovers' and is executed perfectly."
— Kirkus Reviews (starred review)

"Sosa imbues a soap-operatic premise with weight and heart in this fantastically fun contemporary rom-com."
— Publishers Weekly (starred review)

An "irresistibly fun romance spiced with a zesty sense of humor."
— Booklist (starred review)

"Smart, emotional, and sexy, this delightfully modern love story hits all the right notes. Sosa knows exactly what romance readers want—and delivers at every turn."
— Lauren Layne, New York Times bestselling author

"Sosa (*Acting on Impulse*) delivers a steamy and witty enemies-to-lovers romance. Lina and Max's relationship grows against

a rich background of Lina's Afro-Latinx culture, and readers will enjoy the complex cast of side characters."
— Library Journal

Praise for *Acting on Impulse*

"Combine Sosa's gift for creating easily relatable characters and her engaging, witty prose with some off-the-charts sensual love scenes and you have a knockout start to the author's new Love on Cue series."
— Booklist

"The first installment in the Love on Cue series is charming, witty, and consistently funny. . . . [A] sharp romance that begs to be savored."
— Kirkus Reviews

"[T]he book feels both effortless and intricate, in the way of truly great genre offerings . . . and I have very giddy expectations for the next in the series."
— The Seattle Review of Books

"You will not be able to turn the pages fast enough!"
— Fresh Fiction

"With characters that practically leap off the page, and dialogue that sparkles with sass and wit, *Acting on Impulse* is a laugh-out-loud read with pulse-pounding sexy times."
— Tracey Livesay, author of Love Will Always Remember

Praise for *Amor Actually*

"It's almost too cozy and delectable for words."
— The New York Times

"Don't miss this sterling reminder that Christmas and (love, actually) is all around us."

— Entertainment Weekly

"Find everything you love about romance in this collection. . . Each story is certain to leave you with a smile on your face."

— BuzzFeed

"A thoughtful, holiday-themed romance anthology that intentionally highlights diverse love stories and incorporates Latinx Christmas traditions."

— HipLatina

A NOTE FROM THE AUTHOR

Thank you, dear reader, for purchasing or borrowing a copy of Sun of a Beach, my sexy contemporary rom-com novella set on a fictional island in the Caribbean. SOAB was originally published as an Audible Original, and I'm delighted that it's now available in digital and print editions. Still, I'd like to take a moment to acknowledge the audiobook narrators, Sean Crisden and Valentina Ortiz, who delivered spectacular performances as Donovan and Naomi, respectively. If you haven't listened to the audiobook, I highly recommend it. In any case, I hope you enjoy reading SOAB as much as I enjoyed writing it. Now, grab your favorite beachside beverage and hop on for the ride!

For the changemakers

1

NAOMI

*A*s I approach M-Class magazine's inner sanctum, I repeat this morning's mantra in my head: *If you can't beat them at their own game, change the game altogether.*

"Good morning, Naomi," my boss's assistant says when I reach her desk.

"Good morning, Anabelle. Linda asked to see me. Is she in?"

"She is."

"And on a scale of one to ten, how would you rate her mood today?"

"Hmm. I'd say about a four? Breathing isn't a fireable offense just yet, but it might get you a warning notice in your HR file."

"Oof. Figures. But I'm not going to let Linda's mood get in my way. Because today I will *not* be deterred."

"You *go*, girl."

"Unh-unh, Anabelle. Step away from Twitter and retire that phrase forever."

"Sounds like I'm trying too hard?"

"Among other things."

"Noted. Well, head on in when you're ready. And whatever it is you're hoping for, I'm crossing my fingers you get it."

"Thanks."

Mentally swatting away the butterflies in my stomach, I push open the massive door to my boss's office—and trip over the threshold strip as I enter.

Puñeta.

Grimacing at my untimely clumsiness, I quickly gain my bearings and take in my surroundings.

Linda Swanson, a tiny woman with a severe expression and a chilly disposition, sits behind her mahogany desk, a pair of turquoise-framed spectacles resting on her hawkish nose. The intimidating frown dominating the lower half of her pale face is no match for my resolve, though.

When she looks up from the papers in front of her and sees me, she curves her ruby-painted lips into a welcoming smile. Uh-oh, *that right there* is a sign of trouble.

"Naomi, my dear, it's *so* good to see you."

And . . . that's another red flag. In the four years I've been employed at M-Class magazine—first as a circulation clerk, then as an audience development manager, and now in my current position as assistant to the publisher—Linda has *never* claimed to be happy to see me. Sure, I know she appreciates my skills and expertise, but happiness simply isn't a part of her repertoire. She's brilliant, yes, and she'll move mountains for her employees, but she's a grouch in designer clothing. A smart, loyal, grumpy boss—that's Linda. Sidenote: I'd never tell her this, but I want to *be* her when I grow up.

"Good morning, Linda." I approach the guest chair, my damp palms hidden behind my back, and meet her unwavering gaze head-on. "Did you read my email about the circulation and subscription information you requested?"

I'm guessing she hasn't because the numbers, in short, are depressing, and no one ever smiles at the bearer of craptastic news. No matter. I'm prepared to give her the highlights.

"I *did* read it." Linda slides her rolling chair back and sits up straight. "And I see you took the initiative to make some recommendations on how to move forward."

She dons a placid expression, making it difficult for me to guess her true reaction to the suggestions I laid out for her. Linda may not always agree with me, but she values my opinion, a fact that has landed me a place as her trusted right hand. This situation is different, though: Today, I'm advocating for myself.

I sit as gracefully as possible in a skirt that seems to have grown snug overnight—bloating's a bitch with a shiv—and lean forward. "May I explain?"

"Of course."

My opportunity to lay the groundwork for steering the magazine in a different direction and altering the trajectory of my career rests on delivering my carefully worded speech in less than three minutes; Linda rarely cedes the floor longer than that. After blowing out a long breath, I begin my pitch. "I've studied the numbers and those of our competitors, and I think we should consider several tweaks to our editorial focus. For years, M-Class has catered to certain readers, namely, single white heterosexual males with disposable income, but we're not tapping into numerous demographic groups that do and *could* comprise our readership if we catered to their interests as well. I'm not suggesting a complete overhaul, mind you. I know it wouldn't be prudent to make sweeping changes to M-Class's brand overnight. So what I'm proposing is that we test the waters first. Run a few features with a more inclusive editorial bent and see how they do. And I was thinking that I could write—"

A rap at the door jolts me out of my persuasive zone. *Shit*. I turn my head and visibly cringe when the magazine's creative director, Donovan Taylor, pokes his head in.

"Linda, you asked to see me?"

The only man at M-Class who makes me queasy, like *damn-he's-ridiculously-hot* queasy, sweeps his gaze from the top of my head to the heels of my nude pumps and rolls his eyes at me. Yes, rolls them. Like a surly pre-teen. He's also the only person who irritates me to no end. It's a lovely—and frustrating as hell —combination.

"Donovan, come in. You and Naomi are just the two people I needed to see."

That's the third sign of trouble. Why Linda needs to see us both—together, presumably—is anyone's guess.

Donovan grazes a hand over his thick curly hair, then drops his arms as he waltzes inside as if he owns the place. In truth, he doesn't deserve to be at the helm of anything except his own self-admiration society.

He slides into the guest chair beside mine and dips his chin. "Ms. Reyes."

Despite how much I wish it wouldn't, his voice rumbles over me like a storm surge at high tide. All I can do is mentally stand my ground and refuse to be pulled under. I *hate* that this man affects me in *any* way, but I *especially* hate that he affects me in a way that's highly inappropriate in the workplace. Damn him and double damn my suggestive imagination. That tingle that hits my belly and rolls over me each time I see him? It's terrible news. Very terrible, no-good-can-come-of-it-so-don't-go-there news. Returning my gaze to Linda, I acknowledge my co-worker in a curt tone that masks the churning in my belly. "Donovan."

"Always a pleasure."

Our interactions have never been pleasurable in any sense, so I take his greeting as the sarcasm he most definitely intends and address our boss instead. "What did you need to see us about?"

"Donovan, I trust you've reviewed Naomi's report on the state of circulation and subscription rates."

He nods, his easy grin faltering. "I have."

Linda, as both publisher and Editor in Chief, typically keeps the creatives apprised of the company's financial picture, disregarding the traditional divide between their department and the business staff, so Donovan would have received my report as a matter of course.

"Naomi was just sharing a few of her ideas about the direction of the magazine. Go ahead, dear. And please make it quick."

She wants me to continue in front of Donovan? Hard pass. One, he's not interested in my ideas, a fact he made abundantly clear when I attended my first editorial meeting a year ago—at Linda's invitation, I should note. Two, he'd undermine me just for kicks. "I, uh, I think I covered all the salient points already. Happy to share the specifics another time."

"Are you sure?" Linda asks.

"I'm sure."

"All right, well, I'll say this: You've done a phenomenal job identifying the gaps in our readership, and your suggestions are the kind of forward-thinking I've come to expect from you."

If Linda were the type of woman to cheer, I'd stand and fist bump her right now. But she isn't, so I merely smile and nod, thrilled that she obviously agrees with my analysis.

"However, I'm not ready to give up on our current readership just yet."

Linda swivels her head in Donovan's direction. "So I'd like to do something different for the anniversary issue, and I'm trusting you to implement an important part of it."

Donovan scrubs a hand down his face and gives her a long-suffering sigh. Must be nice to take that liberty, knowing there'll be no repercussions for doing so. Linda has a motherly soft spot for Donovan; I wish I knew why.

"You've always given me carte blanche with the direction of the anniversary issues," he tells her. "And it's been in the planning stages for months."

"Well, Naomi's report makes clear that circumstances have

changed. Now we need to readjust our plans to thrive within the evolving landscape."

Donovan gives me a withering glance before he responds to Linda. "So what do you propose we do instead?"

"We're going to publish a special edition swimsuit issue. This December."

I hold my breath for several seconds, only letting it whoosh out when lightheadedness threatens to make me collapse in my chair. My vision for the magazine does *not* include thongified beauties on its cover. Quite the opposite, actually. If it were up to me (and admittedly it isn't), M-Class would cater to a broad spectrum of male millennials who proudly identify as feminists, represent and embrace the LGBTQ+ spectrum, and want real advice about dating (or not) and looking good while doing so. *That's* the version of M-Class I want to write for—and maybe even serve as an editor for someday. To get there, I need to show Linda there's an audience hungry for more diverse content. A swimsuit issue will muck up my plans.

"You're joking," Donovan says. "That's only four months away."

"I don't joke, Donovan. You know that. And neither of you can deny the genius of my plan: For months, a private charter company has been hounding me about trying its services. And it just so happens that they've offered to charter one round-trip flight at a significant discount to us so they can demonstrate their value to our business."

"What does any of this have to do with Donovan and me?"

Linda removes her eyeglasses and cleans them with a soft cloth, squinting at us as she continues to speak. "We're going to take them up on their offer and save the company money while doing so."

Donovan cocks his head to the side and pokes the inside of his cheek with his tongue. After a beat, he says: "We're taking that chartered flight, aren't we?"

Eyes bright, Linda smiles and puts her glasses back on. "Yes, a flight to gorgeous Coco Bay, a small private island in The Bahamas. You, the essential members of your team, given the obvious space constraints, the models, and Naomi."

My eyes bug out as I process their exchange. "Me? Why me?"

"You'll be my eyes and ears on the ground, dear. Or on the sand, to be more precise."

Donovan lets out a low-pitched groan, but when Linda pins him with her don't-you-sass-me gaze, he coughs into his hand. "In other words, you're sending her to babysit me."

"Now, Donovan, I'm sending her to keep an eye on things and make sure we stay within budget."

"Sounds like babysitting to me."

"Sounds like my prerogative as the publisher to me."

Donovan draws a deep breath and gives her a dazzling smile. "Right. Of course. If that's what you want, I'll make it happen."

"No objections?"

Donovan hesitates, his mouth opening and closing in a span of seconds. "Nope. You're the boss."

Linda's expression falls, almost as if she's disappointed he's not pushing back. But that makes no sense, so I disregard the notion as quickly as it comes to me.

"How long will we be there?" Donovan asks.

"Three days. I'd prefer it to be two, but the charter company wants to make it economical for them as well, so they're picking you up on the way back from another charter. Which is fine, right? I can't imagine an extra night in paradise would be an imposition on anyone."

Donovan rubs his hands together and licks his lips. "Works for me."

So this is what it's like to watch a train jump the tracks before your eyes, huh? That's two scoops of shit with sprinkles on top.

No.

No, no, no.

I'm not going out like this. I need to step in and make my concerns known. "Linda, none of this will address our declining subscription rates and dwindling advertising revenue."

She smiles at me—for a record-breaking second time in a single encounter—prompting goosebumps to dot my arms. "Ah, but you haven't heard the best part. We're transitioning to digital, and the swimsuit issue will reside behind a paywall for everyone except our current subscribers."

Well, shit. Charging new online subscribers to see the swimsuit issue? That's fucking brilliant. Consumers are far more likely to sign up for an online subscription than a print one. And with a swimsuit issue as enticement, the advertising department will sell ad space in minutes. Damn Linda and her excellent ideas that absolutely undercut mine.

"What about content for the issue?" Donovan asks. "Have you talked to Seth about an editorial plan?"

Seth Magnuson is M-Class's features editor. He does what he's told, and Linda does the telling.

"There won't be much of any, I presume. And anyway, Seth is too busy to join you. He'll work with what you give him."

Donovan's brown eyes flash with an emotion I can't pin down. Deviousness, maybe? "I see." He tilts his head, his dimpled chin catching the light slipping into the room through the slats in the window blinds. Is his brown skin as soft as it looks? Why are his eyelashes so goddamn long? Must he roll up his sleeves to reveal the corded muscles in his forearms? Everything about him is so damn rude.

"And you'd like me to hire the photographer and models?" he asks.

"Yes. I figure you'd appreciate that fact."

"Given your reputation, I don't doubt for a second you will," I say under my breath, but loud enough for Donovan to hear.

8

"Something just clawed at me," he says, giving me side-eye. "Is there a cat in here?"

"Seems more like a dog to me," I grumble in reply.

Linda, oblivious to the hidden meaning of Donovan's question, sniffs the air in her vicinity. "I don't have pets. Does it *smell* like there's an animal in here?"

"No, not at all," Donovan says. "Must be my imagination and not enough sleep." Wearing a self-satisfied expression, he rises to his feet and brings his hands together in a single, loud clap. "Well, I guess I should get going, then. If we're going to make our internal deadlines, I'll need to move on this quickly." With a smirking glance in my direction, he pivots and strides out of Linda's office.

What the hell? Is this a dream? What am I supposed to do now?

"Don't look so out of joint, Naomi. Donovan will be on his best behavior with you around."

"Forgive me, Linda, but that's not saying much."

She snorts, loudly and unmistakably. Maybe I *am* dreaming, and this is my subconscious highlighting my insecurities and playing tricks on me. If so, I wish I would wake the hell up.

"Naomi, you've been a wonderful asset to this company, and I'd never ask you to do something unless I thought there was a good reason for it."

"What's the reason, then?"

"Honestly? Donovan isn't the leader I need him to be. But I think there's room to grow there, and I'm hoping your killer instincts and business savvy will rub off on him."

"And he needs a chaperone, right?"

"And he needs a chaperone."

"That's not within my job description, though. Nor do I want it to be."

"Well, what *do* you want your job description to be? Because I don't get the sense that you're satisfied with your current position."

Here it is: My moment to lay my cards on the table. No more bluffing. No more hiding. "I'd like to write again. For M-Class this time."

Linda draws back, her mouth rounding in a soft O. "Whyever would you want to do that? Doesn't seem your style."

"I'd like to write for a *different* version of M-Class, one that would be interested in my voice and opinions."

"So you're saying by definition that version doesn't exist."

"*Yet.* The world's changing, Linda. M-Class needs to catch up."

"I'm well aware of that. In fact, I've been thinking more and more about the magazine's future. I won't be here forever. Still, I'm not one to make sweeping changes without putting a lot of thought into them first. Never have been."

"Believe me, I know. But we need to start somewhere. Give me a chance to show you that a revamped M-Class could be just as profitable as the M-Class of old. Let me write a few features. Along the lines I set out in my email. Think of it as collecting market information."

Linda tilts her head and surveys me for a long moment, then she nods decisively. "I'll tell you what. Join Donovan on this trip and make sure there aren't any major snafus during the shoot."

"Sounds like you're proposing a deal."

"I am."

"Okay, I'll bite. What would I get in return?" I swallow hard, not recognizing the authoritative tone in my voice. *You are killing it today, sweetie.*

"I'll give you a shot at a provisional byline in the magazine. No, better than that, your own column. Bring me your best work, and I'll consider running it. We'll see how it goes from there."

Four years ago, I fled my old job after my *pendejo* of a boyfriend—and co-worker—ridiculed my ideas in private and credited his *other girlfriend* with those same ideas in public. The experience gutted me. Sucked all of the creativity out of me, too. And I reinvented myself here. Focusing on the business side of things but always keeping my eye on what was happening on the magazine's pages. For the most part, it's been a comfortable ride. But it isn't enough. Writing's in my DNA, and those dormant chromosomes are slowly waking from their long slumber.

My thirtieth birthday is on the horizon, and I'm done letting the ghosts of boyfriends past drive my career decisions. Linda's offer is my chance for professional redemption, and I'd be a fool not to take it, even if Donovan Taylor's part of the package. With confidence borne from the knowledge that I'm finally taking a giant step toward reclaiming my career, I square my shoulders and hold out my hand. "Okay, we have a deal."

Donovan's a shameless charmer, sure, but I can easily keep him on task and advance my own objectives. Besides, how much trouble can he get into within the limited geographic area of one tiny private island in The Bahamas?

2

DONOVAN

*T*he morning of our chartered flight to Coco Bay, I arrive on the tarmac early, wanting—no, *needing*—to snag the best seat on the plane from which to watch Naomi's reaction to the photo shoot I've planned.

Naomi's unflappable. Aloof. *Judgmental as hell.* Years ago, I decided it was pointless to try to live up to her expectations. It can't be done. So instead, I do what I do best: Get under her skin. Admittedly, I misfire sometimes. Case in point: The day I told her, despite ample evidence to the contrary, that she was a killjoy who knew nothing about cultivating loyalty among her coworkers—all because she'd convinced Linda to cancel the open bar at the annual holiday party. Yeah, not one of my finest moments. In response, she'd tipped her head in my direction, those dark eyes calm and peering past me, licked her lips, and said . . . nothing. Although I wasn't happy with myself, I gathered some useful information from that encounter: Naomi thinks I'm a joke. A colleague who isn't worth her time. Well, today? Today the joke's on her.

After dropping my duffel bag on the luggage cart, I climb the mobile stairway and peek inside the turboprop airliner's spacious cabin, where a flight attendant, a seemingly prepubescent white guy, arranges a bunch of items on a drink cart.

He swivels and waves me inside. "Welcome to Genesis Air, Mister . . ."

"Taylor," I say as I duck through the door.

He holds out his hand, his boyish grin and ruddy cheeks the most noticeable features on his youthful face. Is he even over the legal drinking age?

"I'm Robert, and along with the pilot and co-pilot, I'll be taking care of you and your group today. May I get you a beverage while we wait for everyone else to get here?"

"Water's fine, thanks."

I fold my frame into a window seat that gives me an unobstructed view of everyone's arrival. Though to be honest, I only care about seeing one person's entrance.

The seat's leather barely gives, telling me the plane is new or recently remodeled, a fact that's reinforced by the unblemished cream walls. Unfortunately, the gold-plated accents ruin the sophisticated effect, transforming the mid-size jet into a prop from an *Austin Powers* film. *Yeah, baby, yeah.*

The photographer and her assistant show up first. I've worked with Maggie on a few projects. She's a professional through and through, a veteran with a stellar reputation for keeping her subjects on task and capturing hauntingly beautiful shots. Although she isn't entirely sure what I'm trying to accomplish with the shoot, she didn't hesitate to sign up for the job, knowing from experience that she'd be paid well for her time and skills.

Maggie pulls her curly red hair into a ponytail, then removes her denim jacket. "Thanks for the upgrade, Taylor. My last assignment, I took photos of models in ballgowns sitting on toilets in the New York City subway system." She shudders. "I'm still recovering." Her assistant and shadow clears his throat, and she pulls him forward. "You remember Ian, right?"

Hell yes, I remember Ian. He looks like Thor's twin and acts as if he's Maggie's bodyguard. His unflinching stare bore a hole through my back the first time I worked with him. He may as well carry a sign that says "Stay the hell away from Maggie" because that's his vibe in a nutshell.

I stand and shake his hand. "Good to see you again, Ian."

"Likewise."

It sounds more like, "Eat shit and die," though.

Maggie flops onto a window seat, and—surprise, surprise—Ian snags the seat next to her.

The models, eight of them in total, appear next, wearing strikingly similar travel bags slung across their bodies in a casually-unkempt-but-I'm-actually-kempt-as-fuck way. They look infinitely cooler than I could ever hope to be. I shake hands with each one, joking about my terrible memory and the inevitable mangling of their names throughout the trip.

A voice behind them booms. "Let's get this party started, people!"

Jonathan, the magazine's staff makeup artist, pumps his palms in the air, his face done up with eyeshadow and blush in various shades of blue and sea green—in honor of our trip, I suppose. Sienna, his partner-in-crime and our resident stylist, shoves him out of the way, her eyes hidden behind enormous black sunglasses. "I need a pillow, Xanax, and a nap," she says with a long yawn. "Excuse me for being rude, but I'm not a flyer, and this is way too early for me."

"It's nine in the morning."

"Yes, but nine in the morning when you're traveling to the West Indies means I've been up since dawn." She flicks a thumb at Jonathan. "And this one kept texting me about his wardrobe."

"Stop complaining, Si. Wardrobe is your literal job."

"For which I earn a *salary*, Jonathan. Unless you're paying me, texting before nine is forbidden. Besides, my advice plainly didn't do you any good. You're wearing socks with sandals."

"How else am I going to keep my feet soft and supple so they're beach-ready."

"*Beach, please.*"

These two are amusing as hell. "Now, now, children. We've got a long day ahead of us. Why don't you settle down and settle in. Maybe a cool beverage will help."

Jonathan and Sienna hurry off to their seats, the promise of a cold drink snagging their attention. Not long after, Naomi, dressed in relaxed jeans and a V-neck T-shirt that emphasizes her curvy body, bursts through the cabin with purpose. Long wavy hair frames her heart-shaped face, and her lips, the only spot of color, are painted in a shade of pink that reminds me of freshly spun cotton candy. She looks . . . nice. But I damn well know it's a façade.

True to form, Naomi takes in her surroundings like she's casing the joint for hidden cameras. And as usual, those three little lines between her brows crinkle as she works out what she's seeing. Her eyes narrow into slits when she processes that something's amiss. Damn, this is a joy to watch.

She stomps through the cabin and plants her long legs directly in front of me. "Donovan, may I have a word with you?"

"Sure, Naomi." I gesture to the seat next to mine. "Here's as good a place as any."

Her nostrils flare a bit, but then the curtain of indifference falls over her face. "Fine." She drops into the chair, twisting her upper body to create a cocoon around us. "What the hell is going on? Where are the models for the swimsuit issue?"

Somehow her words make it past her compressed lips. Damn. Her freckles are so close I can count them. One, two, three . . .

"Donovan."

Her curt tone zaps me back into the conversation. Best not to be distracted by Ms. Reyes when she's upset with me. "Sorry." I twist my head around, making a show of assessing our entourage. "The models are here, all eight accounted for. What's missing?"

"*Wo-men*, Donovan. *Wo-men* are missing. Are you seriously planning a men-only photo shoot for the first-ever M-Class swimsuit issue?"

"That's the plan. Linda didn't specify that she wanted female models, did she?"

"Well no, but M-Class is a *men's* magazine, and we both know that's what she had in mind, so . . ."

"I chose to interpret Linda's idea in a way that demonstrates initiative. Leadership, even."

"If you say so, but if that's what you were going for, then carrying out your *boss's* directives would have been a good place to start. Only someone who isn't worried about their livelihood would pull a stunt like this."

"And a boss who respects my position wouldn't yank me off a project I've been working on for months without consulting me first." I know they're the wrong words as soon as her eyes snap to mine. She doesn't need insight into my relationship with Linda. I need to calm the hell down. It's bad enough that I can easily imagine Linda and Naomi comparing notes on me. "She made the wrong call on this one. That's on her."

Naomi hoists her purse over her shoulder, stands, then makes for the door.

"Where are you going?" I ask, trailing her down the steps and out onto the tarmac. "The plane's due to leave soon."

"And it'll be going without me."

Grumbling under her breath, she wrenches her bag out of the cargo hold.

"But Linda asked you to watch over this shoot. How do you expect to do that from here?"

She drops her bag, and it lands with a thud. "No, Linda asked me to watch over a swimsuit shoot for a *men's* magazine, and once again, you're advancing your own agenda. This is a disaster waiting to happen, and *our boss* is going to lose it when she discovers what you've done. I'm heading to the store to grab the popcorn."

"Look, Linda gave me a broadly-worded directive, and I ran with it."

Robert, our flight attendant, swings his upper body out the door and waves at us. "Everything okay out here? The flight unit is making its final checks, and I need to lock the cargo hold."

"Give us a minute," Donovan says.

Naomi licks her lips. The morning's strong winds wrestle with her hair, and she slaps a hand against her temple to hold the strands away from her face. "You *knew* this wasn't what Linda wanted. That's why you never responded to my emails asking to see the vision boards for the photo shoot. And don't try to lie. You're chewing on your bottom lip like it's a dog bone, which means you're agitated about something. You do it *all the time* . . . . I mean, you do it sometimes. Actually, I've only noticed it maybe twice, not that I'm paying attention or counting or anything."

"Are you done?" Donovan asks, amusement in his voice.

"Yes."

"Listen—"

Sienna pokes her head out of the plane. "Donovan, I need to speak with you about—"

"Not now, Sienna."

"But it's—"

"It can wait."

"If you say so," Sienna sing-songs.

I turn back to Naomi. "Listen, you got me, all right? I hid from you. Because we *both* know you would have tried to talk me out of it."

"Exactly."

"Which is a shame because we *both* know Linda's swimsuit issue isn't what the magazine needs."

"Yes, you're right: I don't disagree with you about that. But forcing Linda's hand isn't the answer. Why not just be an adult and *tell* her it's a bad idea?"

"It isn't that easy."

"And going against her wishes somehow makes it easier?"

"No, but it'll prove my point."

She lifts her free hand to her other temple and massages it. "I can assure you, doing something Linda didn't ask you to do isn't going to prove your point." She picks up her bag. "But good luck with that anyway. I hope it all pans out." She brushes past me, the subtle scent of berries and citrus lingering in the air. I close my eyes and take a deep breath. Why does she always insist on smelling like a fruit smoothie?

When I open my eyes again, I realize the momentary distraction has given her time to put space between us. My heart rate hits emergency-room levels. Naomi really has no intention of joining us on this trip. And if she doesn't get on this plane, Linda will discover I hijacked the swimsuit spread before I can show her the error of her ways. Somehow I need to convince Naomi the trip will be worth her time. *Think, Donovan. Think.*

Well, if there's one thing I know about Naomi, it's this: She craves control. Over herself. Over others. Over *everything.* "Wait."

She spins around. "What? And make it quick."

Her response is a mix of a growl and a grumble, and I wish I'd had the forethought to record it. What a fun wake-up alarm that would be.

"Tick-tock, Donovan."

"I can't undo what I've done, but maybe we can do something to turn the situation around."

She drops her chin and tilts her head, using her hand to shade her face from the sun. "*We?*"

"Yes, we. Get on this plane and help me figure out a way to salvage the shoot." When her eyes widen, I add, "Please. I'm begging, okay? If anyone can come up with an inventive angle, it's you."

"Now, why should I be willing to do that?"

Naomi and I approach our work differently, but I can't deny she gets the job done. More than competently, too. And now that Linda's taken her under her wing, she's learned almost every aspect of the business of publishing a magazine. Handing the reins over to her is probably the smartest move under the circumstances. To her, I say, "Because I'll give you complete authority over the direction of the shoot, that's why. Whatever you say goes. And I'll stand by it. One hundred percent. Promise."

The tiny muscles of her face work overtime as she considers my offer. She's more expressive when she's thinking than when she's talking. My lips curve into a smile at the realization.

"What are you grinning about? Is this a trap of some sort? Because if it is, I'll find a way to toss you into the ocean."

"Ah, so you're coming."

"Yeah, I'm coming, on the condition that you do what I tell you to do."

"No problem."

"But if you do anything—and I mean *anything*—to undermine me while we're there, I will slice you into shark bait and sprinkle your body parts into the sea. Turn you into Donovan crumbles, if you will."

If I'm not mistaken, her gaze lowers to my crotch for a few seconds before it returns to my face. I swallow hard, slightly unnerved by the threat that she'd slice any of my parts, let alone *that* one. "Okay, sure, no games. You have my word. Honestly, I'm interested to see what you come up with. Tell me, are your creative juices flowing already?"

It's an innocent question, but her eyes pop open like a jack-in-the-box.

Hell. That's . . . fucking precious. Someone's brain isn't as conservative as she'd like everyone to think. And we're stuck together on a private island for the next few days.

Oh man, I wonder what else I'll discover about Ms. Naomi Reyes while we're there.

3

NAOMI

I will *not* stare at his butt as we climb aboard this jet. My focus needs to remain on the foremost task at hand: saving my own ass.

How could he ever think a men-only photo shoot would end well for him? I just . . . I don't know whether to be angry, amused, or worried, but considering the pounding between my ears, the reluctant grin trying to upstage my frown, and the perpetual quiver in my belly, it's safe to say I'm experiencing more conflicting emotions than anyone should be forced to handle this early in the morning. Without coffee in my system, no less.

No major snafus, huh? Riiiight. If that's what Linda was hoping for, she never should have paired me with Mr. Snafu-upagus.

The immediate solution is simple: I need to stay as far away from Donovan as possible and brainstorm the shit out of this dilemma. Unfortunately, the only open seat is across from him, in an area walled off from the rest of the group. How convenient. I'm sure the seating arrangement is by design. *Donovan's design*.

Resigned to my fate, I make my way through the cabin,

introducing myself to people I don't know and waving at familiar faces.

As I settle into the seat facing my nemesis, our flight attendant runs through the safety procedures and gives us a five-minute warning that we'll need to power off our devices before takeoff. I send my younger brother, Carlos, a quick text:

ME: On board and leaving soon. Will call when I get back.

CARLOS: How long will you be gone?

ME: 3 days.

CARLOS: Did you bring a swimsuit?

ME: Yes. Why?

CARLOS: Hoping you'll treat this like a vacation.

ME: It's not.

CARLOS: You're headed to the Bahamas. It's a vacation. Are the women catty?

ME: Remind me to slap you when I get back. All women are not catty.

CARLOS: I'm just going off what I've seen on America's Next Top Model.

ME: OK, I'll allow you that one. Anyway, the models are men.

Three moving dots appear on the screen, telling me that he's writing, but then the dots disappear.

ME: Still there?

CARLOS: Sorry. I was picking my jaw off the floor. Coño, why am I not on that plane? Take me with you. Please.

ME: Why? So you could ogle the men just trying to do their jobs.

CARLOS: True, true. That would be a little creepy. But wait. Why are they men? This is for M-Class?

ME: Long story. Tell you everything when I get back.

I stare at the dots, waiting for what will undoubtedly be a long message. Pithy, my brother is not.

CARLOS: Cool. Maybe this is exactly what you need. Don't forget to send pics. Numerous angles. Close-ups, too. Please. And have fun for a change. All work and no play makes Naomi a grouchy, hard-up mess. Speaking of . . . I stuck a few condoms in your makeup bag.

ME: Unnecessary.

CARLOS: You never know.

ME: I know. Don't forget to check on Papi while I'm gone.

CARLOS: Will do. Don't forget the pics. Cuídate. Love ya.

ME: Love you too.

I smile as I picture how my brother would behave if he were

lucky enough to join us. Carlos wouldn't know what to do with himself. I bet he'll subscribe to M-Class in a nanosecond now that he thinks its pages will be filled with photos of gorgeous men. Ironically, an all-male photo shoot is precisely what I'd do if I were the boss. But obviously, I'm not. And unless I can devise a theme with the potential to go viral, Linda will cancel the swimsuit issue, fire Donovan, and demote me—in no particular unpleasant order. Showing initiative is one thing; a poorly planned mutiny is quite another.

When I look up, Donovan's leaning forward and studying me, a small smile lifting his right cheekbone. I react like a snapping turtle because I don't know how else to interact with him. "What?"

"Nothing. You're just so . . . intense. About everything you do, even typing a text."

It's unclear whether it's a compliment or a criticism. Even more unclear: Why do I even care? No, that's not right. I *don't* care. I'm just curious. "Hmm," is all I say.

My bag is filled with my usual traveling necessities, and I riffle through it, knowing I'll need gum, earplugs, a pen, and a notepad. The task helps me to avoid engaging in conversation with Donovan, too, and given how annoyed I am about what he's done, that's a benefit to *everyone* on this plane.

The flight attendant glides up the aisle, his arms tucked close against his sides, and bends to my ear. "We'll be leaving soon. Is there anything I can get you before we take off, ma'am?"

"A regular coffee, please. Heavy on cream and sugar."

"Right away, ma'am."

As he walks away, I mutter to myself, "Do I look like a ma'am?"

"Not at all," Donovan says.

"You're still here?"

My head is bowed as I continue to rummage through my purse, so I can't see his reaction. I can hear it, though. If it were attached to anyone else's person, the easy chuckle would be a pleasant sound, but it's Donovan's, and that easy chuckle comes with baggage. The we've-always-been-at-odds type of baggage. Well, no, that isn't entirely true. It's the kind of baggage that comes from being undermined by him in a meeting *that one time* I swerved outside my business lane and ran over his creative toes.

I'd made a suggestion: What if M-Class tackled catcalling? Why people do it. How the object of the catcalling responds to it. The difference between flirting and harassment. It was an editorial decision, one completely within Linda and Seth's purview. But when I described my vision for the layout, Donovan jumped in. "That's another magazine, not M-Class," he'd said. "It's not what our readers expect." I pushed back, but Donovan had voiced his disapproval and Seth ran with it. Linda commended me on my contribution to the meeting, but in the end the idea was tabled and never mentioned again. I'd always been a fan of Donovan's work, so the snub hit me hard.

"You've got me for the next three hours," he says. "We may as well use that time wisely."

For a moment, I meet his flirty gaze and swim in that cocky grin of his. What I wouldn't give to bop him on the nose for trying to charm me. "Considering you're the one who got us into this mess, the wisest use of my time is to ignore you and solve this problem on my own. But if I need comic relief, I'll be sure to call on you."

All the pieces of his expressive face—the dancing brown eyes, the easygoing curve of his full lips, the lift in his brows—disappear in that instant. If I didn't know better, I'd swear I'm Medusa, and he's my latest victim. Damn. My comment stung him. Never in a million years would I have imagined that he'd take my snide remarks personally. This is just what we do. But apparently, I went too far. "I'm so—"

"Linda sent you to babysit me, but that doesn't mean you

need to impersonate her, too. You do enough of that in the office." He leans back and closes his eyes.

Ouch. Now it's my turn to scoop up my jaw off the floor. "I remind you of our boss? In what way exactly?"

The flight attendant returns, carrying my coffee in a paper cup with a lid. I take a deep whiff and let the aroma fill my nostrils before thanking him. Then I return my attention to Donovan. "You were saying?"

He opens one eye, his body still relaxed against the seat. "I wasn't saying anything. Nothing important, that is. Just a product of early morning crankiness. I'm going to take a nap and let you work through this on your own."

With his eyes shut, he removes his hoodie, revealing a royal blue polo shirt that appears a smidge too tight around the cuffed sleeves. Just above the top button, I spy a sprinkling of hair as dark as the curls on his head. It's an inconvenient moment to notice his neck is smooth, with a hint of muscle bracketing each side of his Adam's apple. I hate my view, but I'm stuck with it for the next few hours. Shifting in my seat to angle my body away from him, I lift the cover of my brand new notepad and write, "M Class Inaugural Swimsuit Issue – Ideas."

Donovan clears his throat and shifts in his seat. I drag my gaze back to his face, unable to focus on the task ahead of me. As if on cue, he parts his lips slowly, then he slides his tongue over them and shuts his mouth. It's not a calculated move, I don't think, but the effect is the same: I'm transfixed, the pad resting on my thighs now nothing more than a miniature lap blanket as I clutch my cup of coffee and watch Donovan sleep (or pretend to).

No, he's definitely sleeping. And the longer I study him, the guiltier I feel about the snide comment that caused him to retreat in the first place. I hate that I offended him. Despite our many run-ins, I don't despise the guy. I'm just . . . wary of him. As the two most prominent Black people at M-Class, I once imagined we'd be each other's confidants. But that incident, three years into my tenure, firmly disabused me of that notion. More than anything, though, he frustrates me because he approaches life like it's one big amusement park and the people around him are the rides. Antagonizing him is the most effective way to hang a permanent out-of-order sign around my neck.

Still, the animosity goes both ways, and he's just given me a clue about the reason for his: I remind him of Linda. Riiiight. A twenty-nine-year-old Afro-Puerto Rican from Bed-Stuy reminds him of his middle-aged WASP boss. For fun, I adopt the worst upper-crust accent ever and mutter, *Why, the very idea is positively preposterous, but I'll take that as a compliment!*

I can't help snorting when I'm done.

"Whoa, whoa, whoa. Now wait one goddamn minute. It sounded like you were actually amused by something. That can't be right."

"I thought you said you were taking a nap?"

"That snort is a bad omen. I don't feel comfortable sleeping anymore." Raking a hand through his tight curls, he repositions himself in the seat, raises the window shade halfway, and peeks out. "Come up with any brilliant ideas yet?"

"Still brainstorming."

"Hmm. Nothing on the page. Looks like *brainstalling* to me. And brainstorming is an interactive activity anyway. You can't do it alone."

"I'm still noodling, then." I tap at my temple. "And my ideas are all in here."

"So what do you have so far?"

Good lord. Why is he so damn persistent? Truth is, I've done nothing for the past twenty minutes but contemplate our tense relationship and watch him sleep. And there's no way in hell I'm admitting *that* to him. "I'm still kicking my ideas around in my head. It's a process, and I don't want to tamper with it. But now that you're up, this would be a perfect time for you to explain what you *thought* you'd accomplish by ignoring Linda's wishes."

He doesn't immediately answer, and I suspect I know why. I'm here to do Linda's bidding, and he doesn't trust me not to betray his confidences. I can't fault him for that assessment. My chance at a column with the magazine hinges on a successful photo shoot—Linda's vision for a successful photo shoot, that is—whereas Donovan appears hellbent on sabotaging it. I lean forward to make my point. "Listen, I understand why you don't want to divulge your sinister plot, but let's be clear about one thing: You gave me your word that you'd let me fix this mess, and if you interfere in any way, I'll be the one whispering in Linda's ear that it's time to sack you."

"Tell me how you really feel, Naomi."

I sit back and regard him boldly, unafraid of the challenge in his mischievous gaze. "I just did."

A string of hearty chuckles fills the air, reminding me that we're not alone and that people *do* get along. Just not Donovan and me, apparently. Which is a shame.

"If you must know, my goal was to spearhead an unimaginative and uninspiring swimsuit issue, one Linda would be forced to scrap. Then I was going to convince her to go with the idea I'd been planning for months. A series of letters from up-and-coming sports figures to their all-star counterparts. Think an NCAA champ seeking advice from Michael Jordan or Lebron James. Or Brady Singer writing to Carlos Correa."

I give him a questioning look.

"Singer's one of the top college baseball players," he says.

"Ah."

"Imagine Taylor Townsend writing about what it meant to her to see Serena Williams on the world's tennis stage."

I nod vigorously, picturing the photos that would fill the magazine's pages. "That's a fantastic idea, Donovan. You might even be able to get one of these sports titans to respond."

"That's what I've been working on."

28

"And the *photo layout*. Wow, there's so much you could do."

His eyebrows pucker like an inchworm in motion.

My hands fly to my cheeks. "What's wrong? Is there something on my face?"

"No, no. Nothing like that. I'd tell you if that were the case." He gives me an annoyingly endearing grin. "Probably. Anyway, you really like the idea?"

His tone underscores his shock. Jesus, does he think I'm an ogre? "Like it? I *love* it. It's the kind of editorial content that will appeal to a wide cross-section of readers. What about the photographs? What are you thinking there?"

"I was thinking it would be great to juxtapose those letters with photos showing the up-and-coming athletes at their grittiest. Black and white action shots, so you can see the fire and determination in their eyes, the sweat dripping off their skin. With a powerful pull quote. Maybe one that's similar to something their idol has said."

I'm fired up by his idea. This is *precisely* the type of feature M-Class desperately needs. "The right photographer could capture some magical moments between these sports titans, too. It's the kind of content people would talk about for weeks."

"I'm . . . I'm glad you agree."

"But why not just give Linda what she wants for this shoot, then convince her to implement your idea in another issue?"

He taps the armrest as he wrestles with what to say next, then he blows out his cheeks, as if he's decided to tell me the truth despite his misgivings. "Because this latest debacle makes me wonder if it's time to move on from M-Class. Yes, there's a certain amount of freedom here, but there are plenty of constraints as well. Trying to play a leader when someone is determined never to see you as one is a frustrating exercise, and I'm tired of it."

"If you want to be treated like a leader, you need to act like you're up for the task. Isn't that how it works?"

"So young yet so wise."

"Sarcasm isn't your strong suit, Mr. Taylor." I lean forward to be sure I have his attention. "Look, it's not rocket science. You're treating her professional business like your personal sandbox. How can that possibly end well for you?"

"Maybe I don't want it to."

"You *want* to get fired?"

He grimaces. "It's complicated, okay?"

"Make it simple, then. I'm a captive audience."

"Why do you care?"

"It's complicated, okay?"

Truth is, he's being more open than I can ever recall him being in all the years I've known him. It's forced me to consider how we got to this point and how Linda's decision affected Donovan specifically. Linda didn't ask Donovan for his input; she just changed the plan and expected him to go along. A single atom somewhere in my body sympathizes with him; I need to ferret that sucker out and separate it from the rest of the molecules before it leads me astray.

"Fair enough," he says. Then, without preamble, he adds, "I dated Linda's daughter."

Jack. Pot. I *knew* he'd reveal something that would roll back this cautious camaraderie between us. "When?"

"A few years ago."

I'd been at M-Class just over a year by then. Donovan and I wouldn't have crossed paths all that much at that point. Hmm. The plot thickens. My face blank, I tilt my head and nod encouragingly. "And . . ."

"And when she expressed interest in getting serious, I told her I wasn't a getting-serious-kind-of-guy."

"Is that true?"

"It's *always* been true. I'm charming. The life of the party. The kind of guy you sow your wild oats with."

"You said that out loud, you know."

"I'm aware."

"Just checking."

"Appreciate it."

"So where does Linda fit into all of this?"

"I think she equates my lack of interest in committing to her daughter with a lack of interest in committing to my job. For obvious reasons, it's bleeding into our working relationship."

Yikes. Now I get it. Linda's occasional remarks about Donovan's maturity. Her interest in getting him to grow professionally. I wonder if she's trying to groom him not only for a leadership position within M-Class but also for a relationship with her daughter. What a mess. *This* is why everyone should steer clear of office entanglements. Your heart and your livelihood shouldn't be susceptible to disaster all in one go.

Donovan clears his throat. "There's something else."

"Why am I not surprised?"

"Linda was one of my mother's closest friends."

"Was?"

"My mother passed away five years ago."

Donovan doesn't say how, and I don't ask. I'm struck speechless by the revelation. Of the few things we have in common, I'm sad to learn this is one of them. It actually drains me of any energy I'd usually expend on fueling my long-standing grudge against him. Eventually, I muster the strength to speak again. "I'm sorry. I lost my mother, too."

He leans over and squeezes my hand, and we share a quiet moment in which we're connected both by touch and our shared circumstances. Staring out the window again, Donovan adds: "Linda sees herself as a mother figure. She doesn't seem to get that I'm not looking for a replacement."

Now the dynamic between Donovan and Linda makes even more sense: She pushes; he recoils. And it's all wrapped up in their respective feelings toward his mother.

"Am I the only one who didn't know this?" I ask.

"I doubt it. Most of the old heads know, though. Jonathan. Sierra. All of the editors, basically."

That's not surprising. The wall between the creatives and me is thick, mostly because to them, I'm Linda's enforcer. The person who tells them they're over budget. The person who informs them a feature won't run because that month's issue needs more advertising space. Donovan, by contrast, is their protector, a role I'm sure he adopted to avoid the appearance that he's getting special treatment from Linda. But as enlightening as this new information is, it doesn't excuse what Donovan did. Before I go all soft on this guy, I need to remember that he's in a mess of his own making, and as a result, my own chance at writing for M-Class hangs in the balance.

I pull away from him and rest my hands on my lap. "Here's the thing: It sucks that you and Linda aren't seeing eye to eye on your position at M-Class, but this isn't just about you anymore. Your stunt impacts other people, too—me included. So unless you're prepared to renege on the promise you made me before we got on board, I need you to do your part to salvage this situation. Are we clear?"

"Crystal."

"And just so there's no confusion: Playtime is over."

"I wasn't aware it had ever begun."

"Touché."

———

AFTER WE LAND, an austere-faced white man wearing a uniform virtually identical to our pilots' attire boards the plane and speaks briefly with Robert, who hands the man our group's passports and several sheafs of paper. The man leaves and returns with our travel documents a few minutes later, a thumbs up to Robert his only communication.

"You're all clear to deplane, everyone," Robert says, his eyes twinkling. "Three days of fun in the sun await you."

"It's a business trip," I say to Robert as I pass him on the way out.

"She doesn't do fun," Donovan adds behind me.

"Understood," Robert says, as if that's a perfectly fine explanation.

Whatever.

After a short trip in a cramped van, our group stumbles along the garden path leading to the resort's entrance, where a regal Black woman in a navy blazer and khaki skirt greets us with a warm smile.

"Welcome to Rose Cove, everyone. I'm Celine, and I'll be making sure your stay is as lovely as the weather. There are no more than twenty guests here at any time, so your group will make up most of our occupancy during your stay. That also means you should have few interruptions as you go about the business of taking beautiful photographs. What's even better? There's absolutely no rain in the forecast."

Beside me, Donovan gapes at the scenery. I nudge him and jut my chin out toward Celine. "Don't be rude."

He furrows his brows. "I'm not trying to be but take a look at where we are. This is incredible. The plants are so lush and so fragrant and somehow, they've managed not to manicure the place within an inch of its life." He draws in a slow breath through his nose, closes his eyes, and sighs. "Magical."

Now I'm the one being rude because I can't take my eyes off him. The way he soaks in his surroundings and appreciates them—like he's drawing them inside his body and savoring the sensation? It's mesmerizing.

Oh God.

No.

No, no. no.

If there is one lesson I mastered after my experience with my last boyfriend, it's that those tingly, swoony feelings lead to reckless behavior. One minute you're on the fast track to success in your dream job. Next minute you're ignoring red flags and making bad choices. Not for me. Never again. The next man I date will *not* be a co-worker, and he certainly won't inspire lustful thoughts just by taking a deep breath. Instead, he'll be the kind of man who'd decline to have sex against a wall because he's afraid of exposing himself to germs. I sneak a glance at Donovan's forearms. Yep, that man's a wallbanger. *For sure.*

"This is a villas-only resort," Celine continues, "and we've put your group on the south side, where our largest accommodations anchor the property. If you'll follow me, we'll get everyone registered and escort you to your rooms. The bellhops will take care of your luggage while we check you in."

Once inside Rose Cove's lobby, I can't help shimmying my shoulders to the sounds of Calypso filling the air. Oversize handwoven bamboo fans hang from the textured turquoise ceiling, and a plethora of plants and colorful flowers dot the perimeter, as if the space were made to fit the surrounding landscape rather than replace it. And what do I spy with my little midnight-snack-loving eye? An upscale gift shop that stocks sweet treats. I'll definitely make my way there before bedtime.

Maggie turns to us, a sheen of sweat already glistening across her forehead. "Okay, we've got two full days, and no guarantee that the weather will cooperate despite what Celine said, so I'd like to make use of our half-days, too. If it works for you, I'd like to get started as soon as we can."

"Yeah, yeah, that sounds great," Donovan says as he rubs the fatigue out of his eyes. "But let's give everyone a chance to get settled and freshen up first. I'll see about getting us some lunch."

Maggie nods. "Perfect."

Donovan tells everyone the plan, then drags himself to the check-in counter, where Celine is typing on a wireless keyboard. I stand behind him, quietly waiting my turn.

"Your name, sir?" Celine asks.

"Donovan Taylor."

"Let's see, here," Celine says as her nails clack away. "Ah, there you are. Our bungalows are configured as duplexes, and your reservation indicated that you and Ms. Naomi Reyes—"

"That's me," I say, leaning over and raising an index finger.

"… are the group's co-supervisors, so we've put you two in Beachfront Bungalow 1. It provides both relative seclusion and easy access to the walking trails that will connect you to the resort's main areas."

"Oh joy," I mutter.

"Is that a problem, Ms. Reyes?" Celine asks.

"She's allergic to me. But as long as we have separate quarters, I'm sure we'll be able to manage. Isn't that right, *Ms. Reyes?*"

"Certainly," I say, faking a cheerful tone.

"Oh, that's a relief. Here are your wristbands; they're programmed to open your individual rooms, the clubhouse, and the gym. Now, as for your group's activities, we've set up two tents on the beach that you can use as your temporary home base. If you need us to move them to another location, please just let us know and we'll take care of it right away."

"That's perfect," Donovan says. "Do you have any recommendations for lunch?"

"Actually," I pipe in. "Could we arrange to have boxed lunches delivered to us on the beach?"

"Boxed lunches? With apple juice and everything? What are we, preschoolers?"

"You sure you want me to answer that?"

"Never mind."

"Donovan, don't forget I'm here to keep an eye on the budget. Plus, I checked in with Maggie and the models about this earlier when we were boarding the van. Maggie's on a tight schedule, and the models would prefer a light lunch before the photo shoot."

"Well, haven't you thought of everything."

"I have. Isn't it impressive?"

"It's something, all right."

Celine clears her throat, reminding us we're not alone. "We do have boxed lunch offerings. Someone from guest services can take everyone's orders before you leave here."

"Wonderful," I say sincerely.

Donovan lets out a resigned sigh. "Great."

Ten minutes later, Donovan and I are dropped off at Beachfront Bungalow 1, a baby blue cottage-style house with a wraparound veranda and a white porch swing in front of each guest suite. It boasts two sets of stairs, largely obscured by green leafy bushes, that end at a single grand landing overlooking the ocean. I can easily picture myself sipping coffee in the morning, a hand against the balustrade, as I watch the waves lap onto the shore.

My throat constricts when I glance at my temporary neighbor. Despite a turbulent flight, an uncomfortable ride in an overpacked van, and stiflingly oppressive heat, Donovan looks completely at ease and no worse for wear. I, on the other hand, could use a quick shower and a hefty dose of deodorant.

"It's charming," Donovan says as he gives our temporary abode a once-over. With a smile, he adds, "So I bet you hate it."

I blow out a slow breath. "Actually, I love it. It's your company that leaves much to be desired." Then, with a toss of my hair, I wave my wrist at the keypad, glide inside my suite, and shut the door.

These next few days are going to test my patience like never before.

4

DONOVAN

hen I arrive at our makeshift staging area on the beach, the models—some wearing bathrobes and others in bathing trunks—are lounging in director's chairs, their boxed lunches resting on their laps.

Maggie and Ian are off to the side, their heads close together as they confer about who knows what, while Sienna paces on the sand, her brows knitted as her gaze darts from model to model. Neither Jonathan nor Naomi appear to have arrived yet.

The tension in Sienna's expression dissipates when she sees me.

"Houston, we have a problem," she says.

"Sienna, I bet I'll have a solution."

"You better. Or be prepared for Naomi's wrath."

"I'm always prepared for Naomi's wrath. Why don't you tell me what's going on."

"Wardrobe's the problem. Or our lack of one, I should say."

"What do you mean?"

"Donovan, I packed women's swimwear for the trip. I even cajoled Millie Blanca to send me a few pieces from her upcoming collection. I didn't get the memo that we'd be photographing men. I tried to tell you before we left Jersey, but you cut me off, remember?"

"Shit."

"Exactly." Sienna's eyes widen. "And don't look now, but Naomi's on her way over here."

"Shit."

"Exactly."

"Don't worry about it, Sienna. This obviously isn't your fault. I'll handle this."

I paste on a carefree smile and swing around to greet Naomi.

Shit.

No amount of warning could have prepared me for this sight. Naomi, tortoiseshell-framed sunglasses in hand and a large canvas satchel on her shoulder, is trudging through the sand—in above-the-knee shorts. I don't know what the hell it is about those shorts, but they force me to adjust my impression of my typically buttoned-up and pencil-skirted colleague. Makes me wonder where else she might wear them. A ball game, maybe? Is she even a sports fan? Or maybe she'd wear them to a cookout—where she'd eat and laugh and spend time with friends and family. Does she do that?

"How were your juice box and animal crackers?" she asks.

Yeah. No. I refuse to believe she has friends.

"Naomi, we need to talk."

"I'm listening."

"We don't have swimsuits for the models. For obvious reasons, Sienna didn't know we'd be shooting men, so she didn't pack accordingly."

"Wait. You orchestrated this beach caper and didn't clue her in on your plans?"

"I didn't."

"Grrr. Son of a . . . beach."

"Say what you were really thinking. I dare you."

"Pass."

"Just one curse, Naomi. You'd be surprised how freeing it can be."

"Oh, don't worry, Donovan. I'm plenty filthy in my head."

"Is that right?" I say with a lift of my brows.

"That's not what I meant and you know it. Ugh, I could just wring your neck right now."

"What else is new?"

"Stop distracting and deflecting. We're going to need swimsuits, obviously, but let me tell you what I'm thinking before we troubleshoot that issue."

"I'm all ears."

"We're going to do a spread on being an anti-beach bum."

"A what?"

"An anti-beach bum. Someone who doesn't laze around on the beach. Instead, we'll have the models engaged in all types of water sports. Think water skis, jet skis, surfboards, paddle boards, whatever."

"Okay, sounds great. Uninspired but great."

"And . . . that doesn't sound like the enthusiastic support you promised."

"Sorry. You're right. We'll run with that idea and see how it looks. Fair enough?"

"Fair enough. As for men's swim trunks, I'm thinking the gift shop might have some, and we'll need to line up the water sports equipment. I have some thoughts about who from our team should do that, but I'm happy to consider your suggestions."

Something about the way she says all this gives me pause. It's a test. A test she thinks I'm going to fail. Big time. And despite how much I'd prefer to let her think the worst about me, I can't do it. As to this, Naomi's absolutely right: I fucked this up all by myself. Now I need to take ownership of this mess and do what I can to help her fix it. "I'll get the trunks *and* the equipment."

"Progress. It's a *wondrous* thing to witness."

"Laying it on a little thick, wouldn't ya say?"

"There's no such thing as laying it on a little thick when it comes to you."

"Touché."

"Now chop-chop, off you go. We don't have all day. I'll fill Maggie in on the plans while you pull together what we need."

"Yeah, yeah. I'm on it."

"Oh, and Donovan . . ."

"What's up?"

"Make sure to grab a few Speedos."

———

"THAT'S IT, PAUL," Maggie says, twisting and turning fluidly as she takes each shot. "Square your shoulders a bit more and stand up on the board. Bend your knees. No, turn this way. We need to see your profile. Hang on a minute. Ian!"

"I'm right here, Mags."

"Can you pull up a video of someone standing on a surfboard and show it to Paul? Give him a frame of reference or something?"

"You got it."

Maggie trudges through the knee-high water back to shore, removes the camera strap around her neck, and drops her head on a long sigh.

"That bad?" I ask her.

"It's not bad. It's just . . . boring. If I'm not excited about my subject, the shot isn't going to be all that interesting, either. Plus, everyone's tired. We should probably call it a day and start fresh tomorrow."

"Want me to talk to her?"

Maggie casts a furtive glance at Naomi, who's chatting with Sienna in one of the tents, the rest of the models hovering as they wait for further direction from us. "You're the client. I'm here to do what you want."

"Which means you're here to do what she wants."

"How'd that come about?"

"I screwed up. Promised to hand over the reins to her so she can fix it."

"Forgive me for saying this, but you two are a mess. From the moment we got on that flight, you've been growling at each other like my fur babies do when there's only one treat left. Did it ever occur to either of you that if you worked *together,* you just might make magic?"

"Honestly? No, it never occurred to me. Naomi and I have never meshed well. Our work styles are too different, so it's only tension and more tension. Hell, we barely tolerate each other on a good day. It's hard to imagine any magic could ever come from a stressful situation like this one."

"Oh, you sweet summer child. I hope I'm around when you figure this out. And I hope it happens soon—for both of your sakes."

5

NAOMI

*a*fter a much-needed nap, I walk along the lighted stone path to the resort's outdoor dining area, eventually stopping (and gawking) at a long rectangular buffet table filled with an assortment of foods resting in gleaming silver chafing dishes. Savoring the smell of pineapple and grilled meats permeating the air, I eagerly secure a plate and make my way through the sumptuous offerings: grilled snapper, conch fritters, minced beef patties, peas and rice—I want it all. And oh my God, I spy with my greedy eye the crispy, golden brown plátanos that can be found in one form or another *everywhere* in this region of the world.

Hands weighed down by my culinary spoils and a frosty peach daiquiri, I glance at the available seating and consider my options.

The models are sitting together, their bodies creating a tight circle that suggests they're not interested in interacting with me or anyone else. Yeah, they can probably sense it, too: This afternoon's photo shoot was a bust. If any of them were hoping a spread in M-Class would catapult their career, reality probably setting in by now and they're regretting this assignment.

At another table, the remaining members of our group chat animatedly, the low hum of their conversation occasionally interrupted by raucous laughter. I'm not an anti-social person by nature, but the prospect of spending any more time in Donovan's presence unsettles me, and I hate being unsettled by anything. He's a modern-day rake, and if I'm not too careful, he'll challenge me to climb atop a table and belt out a song. With enough liquid courage in my body, I'd do it, too—and lose my co-workers' respect forever. No, we can't have that.

I spin away from both groups and pivot toward an empty stool at the bar. Seconds away from claiming it, I hear Donovan's booming voice ringing in the air.

"Hey, Naomi, over here. Join us."

I freeze, my shoulders tensing before I remember to adopt the detached air Donovan expects of me. Schooling my features, I face the table and raise my glass. "There you are. It's kind of dark out here. I'm having trouble making anyone out."

No one seems to question my explanation—no one, that is, but Donovan, who smirks at me as he watches my approach through heavy-lidded eyes. Yeah, it's not like the resort's overrun with guests, so he probably sees right through me.

Jonathan and Sienna scoot apart, and Donovan drags a chair from an empty table nearby, patting the seat as though I need guidance on how and where to sit. I mumble a stilted "thank you" and focus on unrolling my cloth napkin and arranging the utensils tucked inside. He's watching me. I don't need to look at him to know this. I sense it as I listen to the others chat about the island and notice he's not contributing to the conversation.

Focusing on my food has the added benefit of ensuring I'm not ensnared by Donovan's steady gaze. As everyone around me engages in casual conversation, I keep my eyes downcast and sample the decadent items on my plate.

"Ever been on a private island before?" Jonathan asks Donovan, his voice more boisterous than either the question or the occasion calls for. "What am I even asking? Of course he's been on a private island before. Probably several. With a different woman at each one."

I look up then.

Sienna snorts, Maggie raises a brow, and Ian narrows his eyes.

Donovan takes a long sip of his whiskey-colored drink, not bothering to set aside the pineapple slice notched to the rim. "Don't believe everything you've heard at the water cooler, Jonathan. I've never dated anyone at M-Class."

"I think that's his point," I chime in. "*Dating* isn't the operative word here."

"Ooh," Sienna says, her eyes waggling as if she's looking forward to whatever fallout may follow from my ill-conceived outburst. "I'm loving this new side of you, Naomi. Our fair leader has a nice uppercut. It's refreshing."

"We're going to have to agree to disagree on that one," Donovan says, his eyes flickering with amusement.

Maggie clears her throat. She's plainly bored with our nonsense. "Well, it's been a long day, and we have an even longer one ahead of us tomorrow." She salutes everyone at the table. "Be good, folks." Her gaze swings between Donovan and me. "And try to be nice to each other."

"I'll walk back with you," Ian says, hastily rising from his chair and jogging after her.

As they walk away, someone increases the volume of the music playing through the resort's speakers from dolce to shake-your-ass-on-the-patio levels.

One of the models, a tall, curly-haired man with an infectious smile, jumps up from his seat. "That's my song!"

"You know how to dance merengue?" I ask.

"I'm Dominican. It's in my blood."

"Boricua over here. I know what you mean."

"Seriously?"

"Seriously."

He puts out a hand. "Manny."

I grab it without hesitation, letting him pull me to standing. "Naomi." To everyone else, I say, "Excuse me, folks. Duty calls."

Manny and I fall into step together as though we've known each other for years.

"Brings back memories of family get-togethers in Harlem," I say wistfully.

"Don't tell me you grew up in New York, too."

"Yup. Upper East Side. You?"

"The Bronx."

"A Dominican who isn't from Washington Heights? Wow. You're a unicorn."

We grin at each other, then he spins me out, and as I circle back to him, I spot Sienna and Donovan joining us on the makeshift dance floor. Manny and I release each other's hands and draw them into a circle, clapping to the beat in encouragement.

I can't help teasing Donovan. "What?!? You're on the dance floor, too?"

"She looked so sad watching you two dance. What else could I do?"

Within seconds, Sienna sidles up to Manny, locking her gaze on him and making it clear he was her true target all along.

I lean toward Donovan. "I think you're off the hook."

"Might as well be. I have no idea what I'm doing."

"Just listen to the rhythm. The song even gives you directions. 'A la derecha' and 'a la izquierda' means to the right and to the left. So move your hips when the song tells you to. That's right. There you go! You got it."

The music transitions to another upbeat song, a mix of the soca sound I've heard in Trinidad and the traditional Bahamian rake and scrape I read about in a travel guide. It's infectious, and I can't help throwing out a few booty tooches. Tyra Banks would be so proud.

"Okay, now *this* is more my speed," Donovan says.

With an ease that sends my brain to dangerous places, Donovan rolls his hips way too provocatively for my liking. Worse, he closes his eyes as if he's letting the music move through him and he's succumbing to the full-body experience. We're inches apart, so close that I can smell the way the outdoors has settled on his skin, a mix of sea and earth so heady my tongue darts out of its own volition, begging for a taste. He finally opens his eyes, and the way he studies my face —a visual caress that promises he'd do filthy things to me if I asked him to—causes my knees to buckle.

He shoots out a hand to hold me steady. "You okay?"

His deep voice warms me from head to toe.

"I'm fine," I say quickly.

It comes out as a chirp, which is fitting since I'm a dodo bird.

Donovan accepts my words, although I know they aren't true: I'm far from fine. Because I'm imagining what it would be like to share a bed with a coworker who generally drives me up the wall. This. Can't. Happen. I *know* better than this. I *am* better than this.

Squeezing my eyes shut, I give my head a don't-be-a-dumbass shake. I don't need Donovan. What I need is a cold shower and a quick exit strategy. "Excuse me. The restroom calls."

"Of course."

I practically sprint away from the patio, the hem of my sarong fluttering at my ankles. When I return minutes later, our makeshift dance floor is no more, and everyone has returned to their respective tables, the group's mood noticeably lighter and rowdier than when I first arrived for dinner.

"I need another drink," Jonathan says, lifting his hand to catch the attention of a server. He's swaying to the music, not quite glassy-eyed, but buzzy enough that another drink will likely nudge his arrow to tipsy on the drunk-o-meter.

Donovan notices, too, and slides me a wary glance—but true to form, he doesn't say a word.

I reach for my own cocktail; it's the liquid courage I need to play my inevitable role as the resident spoilsport. "Jonathan, maybe one more drink wouldn't be such a good idea. It's getting late, and we're going to need to be fresh and ready to go in the morning."

"Aww, stop being a party pooper, Naomi." His slurred words only reinforce that my point *should* be well taken. "Donovan's not pressed. Isn't that right?"

I look to Donovan for backup but can tell from the casual way he's nursing his own glass that I won't be getting it.

"It's fine, Jonathan," he says. "Do your thing. We're in the Caribbean. after all."

"Technically, we're not. The Bahamas is actually part of the Atlantic."

"Jonathan can do his thing in the Atlantic, then. It wouldn't hurt any of us to live a little, no matter where we are."

I pin Donovan with a murderous glare before rising from my seat. "I'm going to see what's on the dessert menu."

"I'll join you," Donovan says.

I don't wait for him because we both know he isn't joining me for a pleasant chit chat.

He hovers nearby as I scan the mouthwatering sweets on display.

Knowing I won't be able to ignore him, I turn his way. "Go ahead and say what you're going to say."

"How'd you know I was going to say something?" The light-ness in his voice underscores his amusement. No surprise. Life's one big game to Donovan.

"I know how this goes. We've been doing this forever. I make a responsible suggestion, and you accuse me of stifling everyone. We're on an island, right? And Jonathan should be allowed to have a few drinks. Isn't that what you were going to tell me?"

He bows his head and shuffles his feet. Ha. So predictable.

"I wasn't going to say *exactly* that."

I lift a plate with a decadent slice of rum cake on it. "But you were going to say *something* like that."

"Yes, something like that. Listen, if you want to work with a team, you have to allow its members a little leeway. You get much more done when people like you."

"Yes, I get it. Your ability to charm your coworkers is impressive. And if you're just another one of their colleagues, they can't fault you for being Linda's favorite. But *I'm* of the view that a manager should . . . you know, *manage*."

His arms cross over his chest in the universal man-child sign of defensiveness. "What do you mean? I manage."

"Yes, and that's why we're on a private island attempting to salvage a photography shoot that isn't at all what your boss asked of you."

"Well, at least I'm doing something productive. In the meantime, what exactly is it that you do? Oh, let's see. I know." He lifts his hands and ticks off on his fingers. "One, nitpick. Two, find fault with everything and everyone. Three, tell people—not, not people, just me—how I'm screwing things up. You're scared shitless to create your own art, so you hide behind criticizing mine."

I jerk back, instinctively wanting to protect myself from this verbal lashing. Why the hell isn't he ever charming with me? Everyone else gets his smiles, his affable laughter, his good-natured winks and his teasing. But what do I get? This . . . bullshit.

Well, screw Donovan. I'm a professional. Always. My colleagues may not want to share a beer with me, but they respect me. And there's nothing wrong with that. Nothing. Donovan doesn't know what it's like to have everyone talking about you behind your back. To have people shake their heads in sympathy because you're the only one who doesn't know your boyfriend is playing you for a fool. He can't possibly fathom existing in a perfectly adequate but unfulfilling career because you're too chickenshit to follow your dreams again. And why the hell am I shaking? And oh my God, are those tears pooling in my eyes? I blink back the dreaded moisture and stare him down.

He clasps the back of his neck and mutters a curse, turning away, then turning back before he addresses me again. "I'm sorry, Naomi. That was uncalled for."

I fight to keep my voice even. "It was. But I'll deal. Look, we've always rubbed each other the wrong way, and being on this island isn't going to change that. Let's just focus on getting the best possible photos we can, okay? That's something we should be able to agree on."

He shakes his head back and forth, then nods sharply, as if he's finally convinced himself that he can play nice. "Right. A promise is a promise. Tomorrow, you'll be in charge. I'll offer my advice, but you should feel free to disregard it."

"Well, thanks, but for future reference, advice isn't advice unless I'm free to disregard it."

The playful smile that spreads across his face almost makes me forget the things I don't like about him. Almost. No, he's still too breezy about his job. Fixated on satisfying his own whims and desires. Eternally focused on being voted the most popular guy at work. And damn if I don't sound like the judgmental bitch he described a minute ago.

"One day, I'm going to win you over," he says. Moving one step closer, his eyes smoldering, he adds, "That's what you're afraid of, isn't it?"

"Wrong."

Not knowing what else to do but eat my feelings, I sink my fork into the cake and shove a few pieces in my mouth. Can't say something stupid if my mouth's full.

Donovan jumps back. "Jesus. That cake never stood a chance."

"And neither do you," I say, though it's not entirely clear which of us I'm trying to warn away. Then I turn on my heel in search of more rum cake. Scratch that. I'm going to need a whole damn bottle of rum instead.

6

NAOMI

The next morning, I wake at dawn, the stress of my gone-off-the-rails job assignment disrupting my ordinarily restful sleep. In a desperate, last-minute bid to draw inspiration from our majestic surroundings, I drag myself out of bed, slip on a breezy sundress, and tiptoe outside, a thin jacket knotted around my waist and my sandals dangling from my fingers. A few steps in and—

"Going somewhere?" someone asks softly.

"Shit!"

I stumble forward, but Donovan quickly settles his strong hands around my waist and shoulder and prevents me from faceplanting.

"Sorry," he says. "I didn't mean to frighten you."

"Right. Because standing in the shadows at dawn and announcing yourself only after I've taken several steps when I'm plainly oblivious to your presence *surely* wouldn't scare me."

"Again," he says, fighting back a grin. "I didn't mean to frighten you."

"Argh. Why do you always manage to make me sound unreasonable?"

He shrugs. "Because you are?"

I spin away from him and skip down the steps.

"Where are you headed?" he asks behind me.

"For a walk on the beach. And some early morning brainstorming."

"You need more than one person for that, remember?"

I wave his comment away.

"Want company?"

I slow my steps and turn around. Donovan's standing on the veranda, a cupped hand at his forehead to block the rising sun. My gaze absorbs his appearance in seconds: the loose joggers sitting low on his hips; his sleepy eyes; the bright white T-shirt; the bare feet. Something about those bare feet gives me pause; after a few seconds, I own up to what it is: the fear that we're breaking down walls that should remain intact. I'm not supposed to see my co-worker's toes, *especially* Donovan's. It's too personal. Too . . . intimate. Clearly, I need to mentally place us firmly in the category of colleagues. I suppose working would accomplish that goal. "Sure," I tell him. "You're the one who got us into this mess. Might as well make yourself useful by serving as my sounding board."

"Such a generous woman, you are," he says as he saunters down the steps.

"You're not going to grab a pair of sneaks or something?"

"Beach. Sand. Bare feet. It's a thing."

I roll my eyes at him, then sneak a peek at said feet. Dammit. They're nice, too. Cared for. Toes filed neatly. Heels well moisturized. Okay, maybe I have a foot fetish. I whip around and take a cleansing breath as I stride across the stone walkway that leads directly to the resort's beachfront. "Let's do this, then. We don't have a lot of time."

I march while he saunters, each of his steps equaling three of mine. I'm in my head, of course, imagining how disappointed Linda will be when she learns what's going on. Today's our last full day on the island, and we're running out of time to come up with a brilliant idea that'll convince her the trip wasn't a total loss.

"Are you aiming to get to a particular place?" Donovan asks.

"I'll know it when I see it."

"Kind of hard to do with your eyes glued to the sand."

"I'm thinking."

"In the meantime, you're missing it."

"Missing what?"

"Look up, Naomi."

I raise my head and jerk to a stop. Oh my. The view takes my breath and refuses to relinquish it. I rest my hand against my chest, the steady beating of my heart thrumming against my fingers. There's nothing but sun, sea, sand, and an occasional gathering of mangroves as far as my eyes can see. The water's crystal clear where it meets the powdery white sand, then it transitions to a brilliant shade of aqua the farther my eye travels. It's so pure, so untouched, that I almost feel guilty about being here. Almost.

"I don't do this enough," I admit.

"Do what?"

"Take in my surroundings and enjoy them for what they are rather than for how they fit around me."

Donovan shifts, the fabric of his T-shirt brushing my bare arm and reminding me that we're doing things together we've never ventured to do before. Absorbing picturesque views. Seeing each other's toes. Talking rather than snarling at each other.

"It's beautiful, isn't it?" His gaze roams over the ocean, its gentle waves lapping at our ankles as our feet sink into the sand. "Reminds me of us."

"*Us?*"

"Yeah. Us. You're solid. Dependable. Steadfast and strong. Turf. I'm waves crashing and thrashing against the shore. Surf."

"Be still my heart. Every woman dreams of being described in such a poetic way."

"You're missing my point."

"Which is?"

"Surf and turf go well together. Aside from being a popular seafood entrée, they balance each other out. Go hand in hand. That could be us. Problem is, we spend so much time encouraging our tug of war when what we should really be doing is pulling on the same end of the rope."

"There's just one issue, though."

"What's that?"

"I'm allergic to seafood."

"Of *course* you are."

"Kidding."

"You? Kidding. This *must* be the apocalypse."

"Watch it, Taylor."

Donovan's right, though, I grudgingly admit to myself. I spend far too much time pushing him away. I've always assumed it was a defense mechanism. To protect me against the probability that he isn't on my side no matter how much I want him to be. But now it occurs to me that something else could be driving my resentment.

I untie the jacket around my waist and place it on the ground. After gesturing at the sand at our feet, I plop down and draw my knees to my chest. Donovan joins me, choosing to sit with his legs fully stretched out.

I take a deep breath. "Remember yesterday when you said I spend my time criticizing your art because I'm too afraid to make my own?"

"I'm sorry, Naomi. I had no business saying what I said."

"No, it isn't your business. But you weren't wrong, either. Not entirely."

Donovan, who's sifting the sand with his fingers and watching it fall to the ground, pauses, his hand hovering in the air before he drops it next to mine. "Tell me what happened, then. Why the switch from writing to working behind the scenes?"

I draw back. "How'd you know I wrote in my former life?"

"I looked you up a while ago. . . And I read some of your stuff. The piece about what men can learn from romance novels was a personal favorite. You have a head for business, but it's obvious that writing's your passion. Honestly, it's the thing that's puzzled me the most about you all this time."

"The truth is, I had a bad experience at my last job, and I needed to take a break."

"A break from the job or a break from writing?"

"Both, actually." After a brief pause, I add: "I made the mistake of getting involved with a colleague." I catch the lift of his brows and mentally smack myself for old time's sake. "Shocking, right? In my defense, I thought I'd found my soul-mate, so the normally risk-averse part of my brain stopped operating. And for months it was great. I had someone who understood my ambitions and encouraged them. He was an excellent sounding board. *Too good*, in fact. I started noticing that another woman writer was pitching ideas remarkably similar to mine. Short story. He was sleeping with us both, although he hadn't shared that little tidbit with either of us. When I tried to reclaim my work, he very publicly declined to back me up."

"What an asshole."

"Yeah, well, it was a lesson I needed to learn, so it wasn't a total loss."

"And what lesson was that?"

"It's better to keep your guard up and lose a few points with your colleagues than get caught with your guard down and lose yourself completely. Blake did a number on me. Screwed with my confidence. Made me question my judgment. And when I got here, I met you. A man who couldn't care less about what people think of him. Someone who charms everyone into accepting him on his terms. I want the same, but I don't trust myself to reach for it. So I hold back. Because I'm afraid I'll make the same mistakes that brought me to M-Class: trusting too much, being too open, assuming people have my best interests at heart. And then the one time I mustered the courage to push through my insecurities, you made me feel small."

Donovan worries his bottom lip as he considers me. He sighs. "The annual ideas round-up meeting."

He knows. He knows exactly what I'm talking about. Which confirms it wasn't all in my head. "That one."

"I was being your colleague. Treating you as my equal. Pointing out that M-Class isn't the magazine you want it to be."

"I didn't see it that way."

"No, I see now that you didn't. I wish we'd talked about this sooner. It explains the steel fortress you've built around yourself. It's impenetrable."

"It's necessary."

"It comes at a cost, though."

"And what cost is that, Professor Taylor?"

"I think it's safe to say it's costing you a friendship with someone who thinks you're one of the most phenomenal people he'll ever meet."

I draw in a long breath, giving my chest the space to fully absorb this revelation. It's as though thousands of sparklers are traveling through my body, brightening places I haven't allowed to shine in years. God knows, my attraction to Donovan is worrisome in itself, but my reaction to his words? It's frightening.

"Meet me halfway," Donovan says, obviously taking my silence for resistance. "Be my friend."

"Friend. I like the sound of that. But meeting me halfway implies you'll be moving some goalposts of your own."

Donovan rises to his feet and holds out a hand. "I can do that."

Taking his hand means something. To him. To me. What would it be like for us to co-exist in peace? To not test each other's patience all the time? I'm eager to find out. So I reach up and slide my fingers through his, letting him pull me to standing. "Let's go see about a location for the shoot, then. That's why we're here, after all."

I voice the reminder as much for myself as for Donovan. Because agreeing to friendship is all I can handle. Anything more is out of the question.

———

AFTER A LONG STROLL along the beach, Donovan suddenly sprints ahead. "What about here?"

Behind us, a sparse grouping of coconut palms sways in the gentle morning breeze. Up ahead, a short dock seemingly disappears into the sea, the sunrise casting a majestic glow of soft oranges, yellows, and golds against the morning sky. "There isn't an inch of this place that isn't beautiful, but it's hard to say without a vision for the shoot in mind. If I knew the theme, I'd be able to picture the ideal backdrop."

Donovan spins around and playfully kicks sand up in the air. When I laugh at his antics, he leans down, rolls up his athletic pants to just below his knees, and slowly runs in the water.

"What are you doing?" I yell at him.

He turns around and walks backward, splashing water in my direction. "Isn't this what we'd see in Sports Illustrated? Oh wait . . . maybe I should wet my hair and shake it out. Or maybe I should pucker my lips and pin you with some over-the-shoulder smolder."

I chuckle, unable to keep a straight face. "Yeah, that's exactly what you'd see. The male gaze in all its glory."

"Keep talking," Donovan says as he draws nearer.

"I mean, you and I both know this is what most media do. Whether it's film, TV, or yeah, magazines. They depict women from a man's perspective."

"It sells, though. Can't argue with that."

"I most definitely can. If you give readers limited choices, some of it will *always* sell. But that doesn't mean another choice won't sell just as well. Unfortunately, so much of our media culture revolves around selling sex to straight males."

He playfully shoots a hand up in the air. "That's me!"

I burst out laughing. The man truly is ridiculous. "It's not a cause for celebration, Donovan. Even less so when you consider that the group we cater to the most is white men."

"Well, shit. That's *definitely* not me."

"I'm aware, but in this case, you benefit from the problem too. Women exist as sources of male pleasure and nothing more. And tons of people are unfairly excluded from the conversation by default."

He ponders this, his brows furrowed like accent marks of concern. "I don't want any part of that."

"And yet . . ."

It's a mild dig, of course. But he can't be surprised by the criticism. He knows very well that some of the spreads in M-Class cater to straight men's penchant for viewing women as sexual beings. The all-female swimsuit issue Linda's expecting would have been more of the same. And now that we have an all-male cast, we have an opportunity to give readers . . . more of the same.

I stumble forward the moment the idea begins to take shape in my mind. "*That's it.* The swimsuit issue could be a satirical look at the male gaze. Put these men in poses you'd expect to see in an all-female photo spread. The water kicking. The closeup with windblown hair and pouty lips. The guy sitting on his heels with his chest jutting out. A stop-drop-and-roll in the sand, even."

Donovan approaches with a quizzical expression on his face. "But to what end?"

"Well, the editorial would try to shed light on the need for more perspectives. Challenge the reader's expectations. High-light that inclusivity *should* be the norm. Discuss gender fluidity, sexual orientation, intersectionality, misogyny, and more. Not just one piece but several."

"If you thought my all-male swimsuit issue would piss Linda off, this would make her livid."

I can't argue with his point, so I appreciate the reality check. "Yeah, I suppose you're right. It was a ridiculous idea anyway."

He shakes his head at me. "No, that's not what I think at all. It's a *great* idea. Much better than my original idea, actually. It'll get people talking, especially on social media. Enlighten some of our readers, hopefully. Plus, it's the kind of thing that could go viral. And advertisers love content that goes viral. Naomi, it's the perfect opportunity to seize the moment and go for what you want. I'll support you one hundred percent."

Buoyed by his enthusiasm, I picture the spread and the copy to go along with it. I could write a masterful piece on the male gaze. Then, if Linda's up for it, M-Class could solicit articles from a variety of writers with the expertise and experience to discuss the many facets of diverse representation. Donovan's right: This could be my chance to show Linda what M-Class could be if we took it to new heights. She may disagree with our methods, but maybe she'll appreciate the results. "I'm willing to give it a shot."

"So am I."

"Oh! And a title for the article I'd write just popped into my head. We have eight models, right?"

"Right."

"We'll call it Ocean's 8. I can even point out the parallels between our spread, the movie franchise, and the lone spinoff featuring an all-women cast."

"Damn, that could be brilliant, Naomi. Really brilliant."

"And I have *you* to thank for helping me literally stumble upon the idea."

"Well, I'm glad I could help. And it just goes to show you: We *can* make a great team."

I smile up at him, reenergized by the possibility that we just might turn this fiasco around. "Finally. We agree on something."

He puts a hand against his forehead, then peers around us, searching for something in the distance.

"What is it?"

"We agreed on something, so I'm looking for the zombies."

"Har-har," I say, then I grab his hand. "Let's head back. We have a photo shoot to finish."

7

DONOVAN

After breakfast, Naomi and I head over to the staging tents. There's a buzz in the air, as if the new direction of the photo shoot has given our team a sorely needed burst of positive energy.

I wish I could attribute my good mood to the exciting direction we're taking, but I know there's only one reason I feel a million pounds lighter: Naomi.

Being on good terms with her is good for the soul. When I'm on the receiving end of one of her bright smiles? Damn, I feel it down to my bones. And when she's bursting with ideas and eager to share them? I could live off that all day. Hell, just working in harmony with her is a gift—and I don't want to squander it.

Once again, though, Sienna arrives to dampen my mood. Wordlessly, she tugs on the sleeve of my shirt and draws me away from everyone.

"Houston, we have a problem."

"Sienna, I bet I'll have a solution."

"You better. Or be prepared for—"

"Yeah, yeah. I know, I know. Naomi's wrath. What's going on?"

"It's Jonathan. He's hungover. Like tossing his cookies, hungover."

"Shit."

"Exactly."

"Is he all right?"

"He'll be fine. I gave him my tried-and-true hangover cure, but for now, he's useless to us."

"I'm glad he's okay. As for the shoot, we're going for natural anyway, so their makeup shouldn't be complicated. Do you think you could step in? I know you've helped Jonathan in the past."

"I'll do my best, but it'll cut into our time. We're down to two hands when we probably need four."

"Do the best you can. That's all I can ask of you."

"That's not all, though."

"There's *more*?"

"Yeah. Jonathan had a drinking buddy last night. Chase."

"Chase?"

"One of the models."

"Ah, damn."

"Yeah. Naomi's Ocean 8 idea is now down to seven."

"Shit."

"Exactly."

"How's he doing?"

"He'll be fine, too. He and Jonathan are recovering together."

Naomi bounces over, her excitement palpable. "Hey, you two! Why the glum faces? I need you to be pumped up about this."

I lift my chin at Sienna. "Give us a minute, okay?"

"No problem."

Sienna darts away as if she's been granted a reprieve. She probably has.

When I turn back to Naomi, she's staring at me, her brows furrowed in confusion.

"What's going on?" she asks.

"Jonathan and one of the models won't be joining us. They're okay, but they had too much to drink last night, and they're not feeling well."

She doesn't do or say anything for a long moment, then she stares off into the distance, frustration pouring off her in choppy waves. "I'm trying to think. How could we have avoided this outcome? It's just so *tough* to figure out what to do when an employee has obviously had too much to drink and you need them to be in tip-top shape for a work project. I. Just. Don't. Know. What I would do in that situation."

"I get it, Naomi. I should have stepped in last night."

"Yes, you should have."

"Let me talk to Maggie and figure out a solution."

"That's okay, Donovan. You've done enough already."

And just like that, our truce is on shaky ground. But that's not the worst part. The worst part is that I let her down. Let myself down, too. All because I wanted to be the good cop to her bad cop in last night's scenario. So yeah, I'll let her take it from here. It's the least I can do.

———

AFTER A TENSE NEGOTIATION, Maggie's trusty assistant relents and agrees to Naomi's suggestion that he stand in for Chase. I must admit, Ian's a wise choice. The brooding modern-day Viking has the height and rugged good looks to pull it off. Maggie, though, who until now has been more fired up about this shoot than any of the others we've worked on together, appears to be having trouble adapting to the turn of events. She can't even look at Ian, so I'm not sure how she's going to manage to take his photograph.

Naomi tilts her head. "I think Ian needs a bit of bronzer. He's looking a little pale."

"Is he?" Maggie asks, her gaze never leaving her camera as she fiddles with it.

Seemingly out of nowhere, Jonathan stumbles forward, his eyes squinting against the sun as he tries to mask the effects of his hangover. "I can fix that." He tries to pat Ian's face with a large makeup brush, but since he's unsteady on his feet, he almost pokes Ian in the eye instead.

"Why don't you sit this one out, Jonathan. Sienna's got it covered," I say.

"No, no, I'm fine, D."

"I'm not giving you a choice. Sit this one out."

Jonathan's wide-eyed gaze snaps to mine, then he backs up and raises his hands, his makeup brush dangling in the air. "Of course. No problem."

The tension's palpable—and I hate it—but I did what needed to be done. As Naomi's pointed out time and again, managers need to manage, and I'm selling myself and my colleagues short if I don't step in when necessary.

Sienna scrambles over to Ian and fixes his makeup. "He's all set."

Maggie clears her throat, unofficially signaling that it's time to move on. "Okay, what's next?"

"We got the water kicking," Naomi says, ticking off the ideas we discussed this morning. "The pouty lips close-up. The guy sitting on his heels with a flower in his hair. Then there's . . ."

"You wanted a roll in the sand," I remind her.

Naomi's eyes flash to mine, then she nods. "Right. A roll in the sand."

"You're up, Ian," Maggie says without looking at him. "I know this is going to be a challenge for you, but you've been on enough of these shoots to know how it's done. Give it your best go, and we'll regroup as needed, okay?"

"Maggie, is something wrong?" Ian asks.

"No, everything's fine. Let's get on with it."

Ian, wearing a tiny red Speedo, strolls to the water and wades in.

"Where are you going?" Maggie calls after him.

"Going to get my hair and body wet," he calls back.

"Ah, shit," Maggie mutters.

When he returns, Ian is soaking wet, and he's slicked his dirty blond hair back with his fingers.

"Should we get Sienna to brush his hair?"

"He's fine," Maggie and Naomi say in unison.

Yeah, I just bet they think so.

"Okay," Maggie says. "Let's get you on the sand."

Ian drops to his knees, then rolls around in the sand a bit, finally settling onto his stomach. He leans over on one elbow and shoves a hand in his hair, his eyes squinting.

"Open your mouth," Maggie says.

He does.

"Now, uh . . . lick your lips."

He does that as well.

Maggie takes a deep breath, then she's off to the races, guiding Ian through a series of shots that brings Naomi's idea to life. Ian embodies his new role as if it's his career, and now that Maggie's into it, he's hamming it up for her, even falling on his back and arching his torso for an off-the-shoulder shot.

Naomi appears at my side. "He's perfect. I'm crushing on him hard."

"Honestly? I might have a crush on him, too."

I catch the barest hint of a smile on her face, but it's gone too soon.

"Naomi, I'm so—"

"It's okay, Donovan. What's done is done. Glad we could make it work in spite of everything."

And then she trudges back to the tent, leaving me alone to wonder how I can regain her trust. The doubting voice in my head tells me I might not be able to.

NAOMI SQUEALS in delight when she sees the digital previews of today's photo shoot. "They're magnificent!" she tells Maggie, wrapping her arms around the no-nonsense photographer and giving her a tight squeeze. "You're a master at your craft, Maggie. An absolute master." She spins around and bows before the models. "And all of you were wonderful, Ian included. I can't thank you enough for being troopers and running with this totally bananas idea." Next, she turns to Sienna. "Thanks for jumping in on hair and makeup."

"Of course," Sienna says. "It was a team effort, and I'm glad I was a part of it."

I know there's no praise coming my way. It isn't warranted. So I focus on doing my job instead. "All right, folks. The sun's going down, so let's wrap up for the evening. Maggie will let us know which of you, if any, need additional frames in the morning. Remember: You're still on assignment, and we may need you tomorrow. Keep that in mind as you enjoy the island tonight."

"What a brilliant speech," Naomi says before she glides past me and begins her trek back to our cottage. "What'd you do with the real Donovan Taylor?"

"I'm trying, okay?" I say behind her.

"By all means, knock yourself out, friend."

"You're itching to start a fight with me, aren't you?"

She freezes, spins to face me, and draws back, her hand gripping the strap of her handbag. "What? I'm not itching to do anything. I can't help it if you do and say things that set me off." With a huff, she whirls around and plods her way through the sand.

None of this makes sense. Yes, I screwed up. I owned up to that already. But we agreed that we'd try to be friends. That we'd try to meet each other halfway. This isn't that. It's very much the opposite of someone trying to meet me halfway. No, it's someone doing their level best to put space between us. And I think I know why.

"It's okay," I call out to her. "I get it now. You need us to be at odds."

"Oh? And why is that?"

With a few long strides, I catch up to her so that we're only a foot apart. "Because it keeps us at arm's length."

Stopping to face me, she points at my mouth and makes circles in the air. "That thing right there keeps us at arm's length all on its own."

The only way I figure I can smooth things over is to open up to her, no matter how uncomfortable it makes me feel. Maybe what we have here is a failure to communicate. "Okay, well since my big mouth is the problem, I may as well make a confession."

"Which is?"

"You scare me, Naomi."

"*Me*? Scare *you*? I doubt that very much."

"It's true. I can't hide my insecurities around you. When you push—for good reason—all I want to do is push right back. Not because I should but because I don't know what the fuck else to do. It's like you're rooting for me to be a better version of myself. Honestly, I'm worried I won't live up to your expectations. Always have been."

"Donovan, that's where you're wrong. I don't want you to be a better version of yourself. I want you to be a *full* version of yourself. Show me all your facets. Sure, you're charming. But I *know* there's more to you than that. The guy who goes to bat for his people? Do *that* without undermining me. The person who kindly and deftly guides his team to greatness? Do *that* without letting them run amuck. The man who passionately believes in his work and is willing to advocate for it? Do *that* with Linda, not just me."

She makes it sound so easy, but it isn't. Not to me. "What if I fuck up?"

"Donovan, you've been fucking up plenty. You might as well swing for the fences."

I can't help but laugh. "You're one of a kind, you know that?"

"So I've been told," she says, her bottomless brown eyes softening as she looks up at me.

"We're good, then?"

"Not exactly, no. There's something I need to say, too: Thank you."

"For?"

"For dealing with Jonathan back there. I know that wasn't easy for you. And rather than show my appreciation, I lashed out . . . because it felt safer."

"Safer than what?"

"Safer than toppling this wall between us."

"Okay, now we're getting somewhere," I say, edging closer to her. If I'm reading Naomi correctly, she's feeling this connection between us, too. Maybe it's always been there. Maybe neither one of us was prepared to acknowledge it. The more we talk, though—as friends, not as adversaries—the harder it is to ignore. "C'mon, Naomi, it's still your turn."

She swallows before she speaks, her pupils dilating as she stares at me. "My turn?"

"To be honest."

"What do you want to know? Tonight, I'm an open book."

"Good. Because I need you to be straight with me: Am I imagining the pull between us?"

She draws in a ragged breath. "No."

"Can you tell me you don't want me as much as I want you?"

She closes her eyes. "I . . . can't."

Her admission rocks me to my core, the tenderness I'm feeling for her rooting me to the spot. I want to spend the night with this woman. Wake up in her arms. Learn everything there is to know about her in the moments in between. She's tailor-made to wreck me in every way. Naomi once joked that she'd slice me into pieces in retribution; little did I know she'd do it just by uttering two words. "Because it would be a lie, wouldn't it?"

"Yes," she chokes out.

Finally, we have a breakthrough.

8

NAOMI

"You're just as scared as I am," Donovan says softly. It isn't a question; he knows the answer.

"Because it makes you feel vulnerable, and you don't like that feeling."

This time, I realize, he isn't just speaking about me; he's speaking about himself, too.

"Be vulnerable with me, Naomi. Whatever this is, I promise you, we'll figure it out together."

It would be ridiculously easy to fall into his arms. But nothing between Donovan and me has ever been easy; my senses immediately register a threat. "I'm not looking to sow my wild oats, Donovan. You said that was all you're good for."

He nods, as if he agrees with that assessment, and my stomach clenches. Disappointment coats my skin and oozes through my body like lava.

"You're right to throw that back in my face. I deserve it. And here's where it gets *really* scary: I don't want to be the guy anyone sows their oats with anymore. . . Because that would mean I can't be with you."

I try to stop the gasp, but it springs from my lips before I can smother it. I don't know where we go after here, but I very much want to live in this moment. With him. I answer the unspoken question hanging in the air. "Yes."

So many things happen at once, it's as though we're trying to break the sound barrier. Donovan and I erase the space between us, my legs encircling his waist as he grips my ass and hikes me up so that we're wrapped together in an airtight embrace. We explore each other's mouths, a tussle of lips that's needy and feverish and makes my head spin. Every brush of our bodies—his five o'clock shadow against my cheek, my nipples grazing his chest—stings like a bite that can only be soothed by more. More him. More us. More everything.

Somehow Donovan manages to walk us to the bungalow. Instead of leading us to one of our rooms, he pauses at the top of the steps, deposits me on the landing, and drops to his knees — on a step that places his face directly in front of . . . *oh my*. We're shielded from curious eyes by the staircase's white balusters and a thick cluster of elderflowers, but I sneak a peek at our surroundings just to be sure.

"What are you doing?" I ask in an embarrassingly breathy voice.

"I want you wild for me, and I don't want to take another step until I can taste you. Would you like that?"

"Oh God, I think I just came."

"Is that a yes?"

"Yes, damn you. Yes."

His hands are shaking as he slides my skirt up, up, up, until it's bunched at my waist, the sticky air kissing my skin. Letting out a harsh breath, he circles his index fingers from the tops of my thighs to my knees, then gently spreads my legs and devours me with a lusty gaze. "Beautiful. Just like I knew you would be."

"Donovan, I need to touch you. Please."

He raises his torso and removes his shirt in one fluid move, his eyes hungry despite the calmness in his voice. "Better?"

"*So* much better."

Donovan's broad chest is dusted with hair and made for my touch. Glorious, indeed. Unable to resist him, I do a little exploring of my own, trailing a finger from his belly button, across his pecs, and ending with a flick of his nipples that causes him to shudder.

"Two can play at that game," he says, his dark gaze boring into mine.

I expect him to mimic my ministrations, but Donovan has his own mind, and I'm so very glad he does. Placing one hand on the step, he leans forward, and grazes his knuckles down the seam of my pussy, then retraces his journey with his middle and index fingers. "Sweet Jesus, your panties are soaked." He tugs on my bikini underwear. "Let's get these off. I want all that goodness on my face."

I whimper, absorbing his filthy words as a promise he's prepared to keep, anticipation making me needy. Greedy. Beside myself with longing.

After he helps me remove my underwear, he raises his torso and stares. "Ah, Naomi. Look at you. You're glistening."

"Donovan, *please.*"

"Well, how can I refuse when you ask so nicely?"

He rearranges the impressive erection straining against his pants, discomfort etched in the dips and planes of his face, then sinks between my thighs. He presses a soft kiss against my mound, and a tear rolls down my face. I'm a network of muscles stretched to the breaking point. A bundle of nerves on override. And when his tongue travels softly along my center, it leaves a trail of scorching heat in its wake.

"Oh God, oh God, Donovan. That's so fucking good. Keep doing that, please. Right there, yes."

Somewhere in the recesses of my mind, a warning material-izes: *Enjoy this, Naomi. But not too much. This isn't safe.* I push the thought away. I've been doing safe for four years, and I prefer this. God, I crave *this.* Slowly, I shed my inhibitions, my need to keep him at a distance. It's as though I'm giving myself permission to truly live.

Donovan makes love to my clitoris. Butterfly kisses. Gentle laps. Strong flicks. He does it all. Nice and slow, then furiously fast. I arch my back and raise my ass off the landing. Donovan follows my movements, latched onto my body and hellbent on destroying me, his moans echoing mine.

Astonishingly, he never comes up for air.

"Oh, that's it, Donovan. I'm close. So *fucking* close."

He treats my encouragement as a rallying cry. Redoubling his efforts and sliding two fingers inside my channel. The tingling builds and builds and builds, until it bursts through me, a mile-high wave cresting then crashing against the shore. Silence reigns, as if my ears are stuffed with cotton. And I see stars. Above me. Behind my eyelids. Everywhere. I blink hard, trying to bring the world around me back into focus.

His glorious chest rising and falling, Donovan caresses my breasts through the thin material of my bodice and watches my return to earth. "There you are."

"Here *we* are."

I sit up slowly, then I lean into him and trace his dick through his joggers. Everything about this evening is drugging my senses: the scent of my arousal; the crisp bite of ocean air tickling my skin; the turbulent rhythm and crescendo of the waves washing onto the shore; the way Donovan pulses against my palm.

I slip under his waistband and circle my fingers around his length. He's thick. Long. Deliciously hard. Searingly hot. Each thrust will leave no part of my pussy untouched. I want that feeling. "Donovan, I need you inside me."

He groans, his eyes and lips glossy with desire, but all too soon he grimaces, his jaw tightening in frustration. "Damn, I want to be inside you, too, but I don't have protection."

"Then it's a good thing I came prepared," I say, continuing to stroke him.

"Well, then, what the hell are we waiting for? Let's get your fine self to a bed."

"A bed? How trite. You don't want to fuck me right here?"

"Listen, if you ever get a splinter in your ass, I'll happily remove it with my teeth, but how about we save that for another day?"

"Good call."

Donovan rises off his knees and pulls me to standing. I'm sensitive everywhere. Even the sensation of falling fabric skating over my skin elicits a frisson of need. Before long, I'm drawn into the circle of Donovan's strong arms, and my mouth instinctually seeks his. We kiss as he walks me backward to the door of my suite, prolonging a connection that's still so new it seems unreal. Without looking, I wave my wrist in front of the keypad, then drag him inside.

We strip each other naked in seconds, then I'm diving for the strip of condoms I carelessly tossed on the sofa table because I never imagined I'd need it during this trip. *Bless you, Carlos.*

"Are we really doing this?" I ask Donovan, a tinge of wonder in my voice as I saunter toward him.

"Please, please, please tell me we are."

The urgency in his voice spurs me to action. I open the foil packet, remove a condom, then toss the rest of the strip onto the couch. "May I?"

"You sure as hell may."

Donovan grips his dick, angling it as if he's my sexual apprentice and wants to study my method for rolling on protection. When I'm done, I take his hand, poised to draw him to the bedroom twenty feet away.

"Too far," he growls as he grabs my ass and lifts me against him. "Baby, I need to be inside you now."

"What did you have in mind?"

Without a word, he strides a few steps, carrying me with

him. When my back hits the wood paneling and he slides the crown of his cock along my center, I have my answer.

I *knew* it: The man's a wallbanger.

———

OUR LAST MORNING on Coco Bay, I wake to Donovan's soft lips brushing my cheeks and forehead. I snuggle into him, not wanting the bliss of the past hours to end.

"Sorry to cut this short, but Maggie needs a few more frames before we leave."

"Ugh. Who does she think she is wanting to do her job properly? The nerve of that woman."

Donovan grins as he climbs out of bed, then he saunters to my side, the muscles of his powerful thighs hypnotizing me the moment he's in motion. He coaxes me out of the cocoon of the bedspread and pulls me to standing. There's something about his posture, though, the way he's gnawing on his bottom lip, that alerts me to his inner turmoil.

"What's wrong?"

Thrusting his hands in my hair, he groans as he plants his mouth on mine. When we separate, he says, "Dammit, I want to make love to you again, but we don't have time. Not for what I have in mind."

"Raincheck?"

He takes a shaky breath, his eyes softening. "You're not regretting what we did?"

"I'm not. Are you?"

"I'm only regretting that we didn't get here sooner."

"Maybe this is how it was meant to be."

"Maybe . . . But I want to make a few things clear."

"What's that?" I ask, hating the hesitation in my voice.

"I think you're the future of M-Class, whether we're together or not. You have the drive, the ideas, and the ability to keep everyone in line. I don't want to smother any of that. And

I don't want to take credit for any of that, either. I promise to have your back—no matter what."

"Thank you. It means so much to hear you say those words. Dating a co-worker isn't something I thought I'd ever do again. You just made me feel a thousand times better about taking that risk."

More importantly, I'm finally ready to stop blaming myself for being in a toxic relationship. No, the blame falls squarely on my ex-boyfriend. *He's* the one who didn't deserve my trust. *He's* the one who broke it.

"I'm a patient man, Naomi. We can take all the time you need."

"So we'll take baby steps, then? See how it goes?"

"I like that plan."

"And we won't be announcing anything to anyone."

"Of course. My lips are sealed."

"That's a shame. I was hoping you'd kiss me again."

"I could be persuaded to unseal them. For you. *Only* for you."

"Oh good. I really like the sound of *that* plan."

Then he kisses me. And this kiss is full of promise. Just like us.

9

DONOVAN

*L*inda's gaze remains fixed on the proofs of the magazine spread I sent her last night.

"I can explain."

She lifts her head and spears me with a harsh gaze. "Is this a joke?"

"It's an idea. An excellent one, too."

"Where are the women?"

"There aren't any. That's the point."

She drums her fingers on the desk as she studies me. "Yes, I read the editorial content Naomi drafted, so I was able to put two and two together." She flips through the pages. "But I was wondering when I'd see the photo spread I asked for. The one this company paid a lot of money for. The one you were tasked to supervise. You can imagine my surprise when I didn't see it."

"We went in a different direction. I hired the models we needed."

"Ah. So you changed the direction of the shoot before you got on the plane. Knowing this wasn't what I asked for."

There's no denying it. I need to fess up to what I did. "Yes."

"Why?"

"Honestly? I was angry—at first. You made a momentous

decision without any input from me. As if I were your lackey. As if my creative contribution to this magazine wasn't deserving of your respect."

She lifts a brow. "And this is how you show me otherwise? By disregarding my wishes?"

"I wanted to make a statement."

"Quite the statement, I'd say. The kind that could get you fired. The kind that could get Naomi fired as well."

This isn't Naomi's fault. And I'll do anything to make sure she gets out of this unscathed. "Ms. Reyes objected to the shoot from the outset."

"Then how'd you convince my steadfast assistant to go along with your shenanigans?"

———

NAOMI

MY FIRST ORDER of business is to drop to Linda's feet and ask for forgiveness. Well, hopefully something less dramatic will suffice, but I'm willing to embarrass myself if it means she won't take her anger out on Donovan and me.

When I get to her office, I pause just outside her open door and immediately register that she isn't alone. Donovan's deep voice carries into the hall.

"Naomi didn't even want to get on the flight. Luckily, I changed her mind. I know it's unconventional, but you must admit that if we go through with this spread, M-Class will get the kind of social media coverage we've always dreamed of."

"And the idea to focus on the male gaze? Who came up with that?"

Donovan hesitates, and my heart constricts as if it's trying to arrange itself into a knot that can't be untied. The idea was mine. Why wouldn't he just tell her so? Memories of past betrayals bubble to the surface. Is he prepared to take credit for my concept? Would he stoop so low?

I shake my head and pat a hand against my roiling stomach. No, the man who held me in his arms and said he'd have my back no matter what would never do such a thing. I may not know everything, but I know Donovan's a good man.

"It depends," Donovan continues.

"On?"

"If you like the idea, then it was one hundred percent Naomi's idea. If you don't like it, then it was one hundred percent mine."

"Why, Donovan," Linda says, her voice pleasantly surprised. "Are you putting someone's well-being before your own? Taking one for the team, so to speak?"

"I'm taking one for Naomi, specifically. If it's necessary."

"Your mother would be proud."

"Let's leave her out of this."

"I don't really think that's possible, do you?"

He sighs. "No, I suppose it isn't."

"I made her a promise, you know. That I'd watch out for you."

"I don't need another mother, though."

"No, you don't. Think of me as your mentor instead. As for the runaway photo shoot—"

I can't let him do this alone, so I push open the door to Linda's office—and stumble across the threshold strip. Again.

Puñeta.

"Ah, Naomi, come in. You and Donovan are just the two people I needed to see."

"Linda, I know this isn't what you wanted, but—"

She raises a hand in the air, and I snap my mouth shut.

"What the two of you seem to have forgotten is that I'm the publisher of this magazine. And what I say goes."

Donovan and I exchange a worried glance and step closer together.

"Can one of you tell me what I'd hoped to accomplish during this trip to Coco Bay?" our boss asks.

"A photo shoot for M-Class's inaugural swimsuit issue?" I offer.

"Yes. Anything else?"

I shrug; Donovan stares straight ahead, looking past Linda.

She sighs. "I wanted two of my most promising employees to figure out how to work together. Because I had a feeling if they did, they'd make a remarkable team."

Donovan's head snaps back.

"So I'd say the trip was partially successful. Now our task is to figure out how to make this right. And the only way I figure we can do that is if Donovan returns to Coco Bay and supervises the photo shoot I'd originally envisioned."

Deflated by her decision, I let out an exasperated breath and try one last time. "Linda, we have the chance to do something really special here. To move the magazine in a direction that will excite readers and advertisers." I point at Donovan. "And did you know you're sitting on a gold mine of ideas here? He's formulated a concept for a sports heroes feature that will be talked about for years."

"I told her, Naomi."

"Don't worry, dear," Linda says. "Donovan will get his sports spread soon. Right now, though, we need to focus on December."

"And you still want to go ahead with a swimsuit edition?" I ask.

"I do," Linda says.

"*Why?*"

"You misunderstand me, Naomi. The photoshoot I'm envisioning will enhance your editorial on the male gaze, not detract from it. Picture this: The first half of the magazine will be what one might expect from a swimsuit issue in M-Class, and then the Ocean's 8 spread and editorial will be featured in the second half. Plus, it occurs to me that if you haven't done so already, a second trip gives us an opportunity to photograph transgender models as well. Think of the impact. The buzz. Show them the default, *then* upend it. Give them what they're used to, *then* show them what's missing."

Linda Swanson's a beast in the best possible way, and I'm in awe of the way her mind works. "Oh, that's brilliant, actually."

"I know."

"Linda, I can't thank you enough for giving us this chance."

"Thank *you* for getting me excited about M-Class again. I can picture your vision, and I like what I see. Mind you, I'm not making any promises about a complete overhaul. Let's just see how this lands."

Donovan clears his throat, then asks: "So you're entrusting me to return to Coco Bay? Even after everything I've done?"

"I am. Because I'm seeing the signs of the leader I always knew you could be. And I think you're ready to step up . . . given the personal significance of this assignment."

Donovan swallows. "Personal?"

Linda looks between Donovan and me, a knowing grin making my heart gallop. Oh, God. She knows we're a couple. Or suspects it. Or at the very least, thinks we're into each other. Who the hell knows? Whatever she's thinking, it probably isn't far off from the truth, and I just want to grab the end of her antique area rug, roll myself up in it, and make a Naomi burrito with embarrassment sauce on the side.

"I just assumed you'd want to see this project through to the end," Linda explains.

"I would. I definitely would. But I'd like Naomi to travel with me. Uh, to collaborate on the assignment. If she wants to, of course."

"What do you say, Naomi? Would you like to return to Coco Bay with Donovan?"

Hell yes, I would, I think to myself. To Linda, I say: "I think that's a great idea."

Linda smiles. "Excellent. Maybe you could spend some of

that time brainstorming ideas for your new *provisional* column in M-Class."

The internal screaming commences in my head. "Seriously?"

"Seriously."

"Can I fist bump you?"

"You cannot."

"Right. Okay. Well, thanks for the opportunity. I won't let you down. *We* won't let you down."

Linda's gaze lowers to the papers in front of her. "That'll be all, you two."

We rush out of Linda's office and scramble inside the first available elevator. Luckily for us, it's empty.

I fist Donovan's dress shirt and walk him into a corner. As soon as the doors slide shut, he wraps his arms around me, and our mouths meet. It's a sweet kiss. Whisper soft. Unhurried because we know there's plenty of time for more.

When our mouths separate, I snuggle into him and stroke his jaw. "You had my back in there."

"I always will. Promise."

"And now it looks like we're going to get that raincheck sooner than we anticipated."

"Indeed. Want to help me pick out a few Speedos?"

"Sorry, Donovan. You won't be needing them."

He treats me to a devilish grin. "Let the beach games begin, then."

THE END

KEEP READING FOR A SNEAK PEEK AT
MIA'S NEXT FULL-LENGTH RELEASE,
THE STARTER EX
COMING IN 2024!

———

PROLOGUE

VANESSA

*I*t started out as a joke. In my junior year of college. Red flags: 2. Vanessa: 0.

My roommate at Penn's International House, Elena Fernández, a well-off Spaniard who was fluent in two languages but skilled at cussing in five, complained that she'd been unable to snag the attention of her latest boy crush. He seemed mildly interested, she explained, and they'd gone on a few dates, but she couldn't close the deal (her words, not mine). What she wanted was a boyfriend. What *he* wanted wasn't entirely clear.

One evening, Elena and I sat at the table in the living room of our two-bedroom campus-adjacent apartment, noshing on jamón, albondigas, and patatas bravas. Elena was an excellent cook; many of the international students were. Indeed, the high probability that I could sponge off their scraps factored heavily into my decision to select International House as my top choice in the school's emergency housing lottery.

Minutes into stuffing our faces, Elena ventured into uncommon territory: asking for someone else's opinion. "What would you do if you were me, Vanessa?"

I took a sip of water before I spoke. "Honestly? I'd find another crush."

I didn't understand why this was such a big issue. College

boys back then were as interchangeable and as ubiquitous as off-brand iPhone chargers.

"But I *like* him," she said, her eyes pleading with me to devise a solution.

"The thing is," I said in between bites. "He needs a push in your direction."

"Get him jealous, you mean?" she asked, her eyes wide and creepily unblinking.

"Nah, that's not something you want to encourage."

"So what, then?"

I thought about it for a second, then casually dropped this gem: "You know what would be downright Machiavellian? If you could manufacture the world's worst girlfriend to date him for a while. Then, when she's made his life miserable and he's hit rock bottom, you can swoop in and save the day. Be the breath of fresh air he so desperately needs."

Blissfully unaware of the wheels turning in Elena's brain, I chomped on fried potatoes while she picked at her food.

Suddenly she straightened in her chair and set her plate aside. "It's a brilliant idea, actually."

"What?" I asked, my eyebrows snapping together. "No, it isn't. I was *joking*."

"Joking or not, I think you're absolutely right. And I want *you* to be the girlfriend."

I cackled. I wheezed. My eyes welled up with tears. Until I realized Elena wasn't joining in on my amusement. "Oh shit. You're serious?"

"Very."

I scoffed as I brought my dirty dish to the sink, the ratty sweatpants I adored hanging off my curvy hips. "Absolutely not."

"I'll pay you."

Insert the proverbial record scratch.

I'm ashamed to say the prospect of getting paid made me pause. After all, I was a scholarship student living off the few work-study hours I'd been fitting into a jam-packed schedule of classes and frequent weekend trips to New York to help my overworked parents run a bodega in our East Harlem neighborhood. Not that Elena knew any of this.

Making sure to mask any eagerness in my voice, I asked, "How much are we talking about?"

She shrugged. "For two to three weeks of your time? Does a thousand dollars per week sound fair? We can see where we stand after that."

My heart galloped in my chest. Three thousand dollars. With the possibility of extra cash if the assignment proved to be more challenging than expected. Damn, I could do *so* much with that money. Buy books for next semester. Send most of it to my family. Not kiss my roommate's ass in order to eat a decent meal for a month or two. Which reminded me: "Kissing?"

She narrowed her eyes. "If you must. No fooling around, though, and definitely no sex."

"Oh, you don't have to warn me about that."

But teasing was fair game, it seemed. And hey, I could be coy. I certainly could be a bitch. Someone's worst nightmare? Sin duda. These were my personality traits in a nutshell, so the assignment wouldn't be a stretch by any means. In fact, this would be a cinch.

Well, that's what my overconfident and underdeveloped 20-year-old brain reasoned, at least. So Elena and I shook hands and thus began my lucrative college side gig.

By the time I graduated with a degree in business from Wharton, I'd served as the starter ex for ten struggling-to-solidify relationships. Bonus? I never had to explain why I wasn't interested in dating anyone—because I *was* dating. Sort of.

Yes, I should have kept this highly problematic venture firmly in my past. But I didn't. And now I'm screwed. What follows is my pathetic story. You're going to want to grab some popcorn for this one.

Side note (in case you were wondering): A few years ago, Elena and her boy crush got married in a lavish waterfront ceremony at Penn's Landing. They didn't invite me to the wedding.

―――――

Keep an eye out for The Starter Ex in 2024!

KEEP READING FOR AN EXCERPT FROM
THE WORST BEST MAN
HARPERCOLLINS PUBLISHERS (2020)

———

PROLOGUE

The Stockton Hotel
Washington, DC
Three Years Ago

MAX

*M*y phone's text tone chirps like a robin—which fails to prepare me for the clusterfuck on the screen.

> Andrew: Everything you said last night made sense, M. Thanks to you, I can see the truth now. I can't marry Lina. Need you to break the news. Don't worry, she'll handle it with class. Going to disappear for a few days while I get my head straight. Tell Mom and Dad I'll call them soon.

I'm too young and hungover for this shit.

Using the few brain cells that survived the effects of yesterday's bar crawl, I try to synthesize the limited information in my possession. One, my older brother, Andrew, the quintessential people pleaser and a man who does everything according to plan, is due to get married this morning. Two, he's not in our hotel suite, which means he fled the premises after I crashed last night. And three, he never jokes about anything; the stick permanently lodged up his ass prevents him from experiencing fun. No matter how I move them, the pieces of this puzzle refuse to fit together.

Could this be a case of Andrew's dormant (and terrible) sense of humor suddenly waking up? God, I sure hope so.

I fight my way out of the bedsheet twisted around my torso, sit up, and type a quick reply.

> Me: This isn't funny. Call me. Right now.

He doesn't respond, so I ring his cell. When the call goes straight to voicemail, I accept that Andrew doesn't want to be reached and wish him a speedy trip straight to hell.

Don't worry? She'll handle it with class? My brother's a bone-head if he thinks Lina won't flip out when she discovers he isn't showing up today. Easily imagining the bride's devastated reaction, I focus on the two sentences in Andrew's text that make me especially queasy: *Everything you said last night made sense, M. Thanks to you, I can see the truth now.* Problem is, I can't remember much about the prior evening—an entire bottle of Patrón tends to affect a person's short-term memory—let alone recall what bullshit I may have said to my brother during his final hours of bachelorhood. If I had to guess, though, I probably claimed that remaining single was preferable to getting married and acted as if I'd thoroughly beaten him in the game of life.

I'm twenty-five. He's my brother. This is what we do.

Christ. I flop back onto the mattress and contemplate my next move. Someone needs to clue in the bride. My mother's *not* an option. She's tactless. At my parents' twentieth-anniversary celebration, she told my grandmother Nola—and a roomful of their guests—that her only hesitation in marrying my father had been a concern that he was a mama's boy, an affliction my mother attributed to the extended period Grandma Nola had let him drink from her tit. Direct quote. My father, for his part, would throw on his investigative reporter hat and engage in an invasive truth-finding mission, all in service to discovering why my brother had bailed on his fiancée. Dad's heavy-handed behavior will only aggravate the situation. I know this firsthand—it's one of the reasons my parents divorced a year ago. Since my big mouth is partly responsible for triggering this unfortunate chain of events, I'm the obvious choice. But damn, I don't want to be.

Massaging my throbbing temples, I drag myself out of bed and limp my way to the bathroom. Minutes later, as I'm brushing my teeth and ignoring my scruffy, red-eyed reflection in the mirror, the phone chirps again. *Andrew.* I spit out a capful of mouthwash, dart back into the bedroom, and swipe my phone off the nightstand—only to be disappointed by my father's message.

> Dad: Get your asses down here. Your brother's going to be late for his own wedding if he's not here in five.

Everything inside me freezes: atoms, blood flow, the whole shebang. I might even be clinically dead. Because on top of everything else, I overslept, effectively destroying my chance to divert the guests before they arrive and adding another layer to this shit cake of a day.

The blare of the hotel's digital alarm clock yanks me out of my stupor and pummels my skull. I slam a hand down on the *off* button and squint at the tiny snooze icon mocking me in the corner of the display. You know what? I'm never drinking again. No, wait. That's an empty promise if ever there was one. Special occasions. Yes, that'll work. Going forward, I'll only drink on special occasions. Does informing a bride that her groom won't be showing up for the wedding qualify as one such occasion? Probably not. Do I want it to? Absofuckinlutely.

———

LINA

PITY. That's what I see in Max's whiskey-brown eyes. In his dejected stance. In the way he's struggling to conceal a pout.

I motion him inside the dressing suite. "What's going on?"

My tone of voice is exactly as it should be: calm and even. In truth, I regularly monitor my daily emotional output the way some people track their daily caloric intake, and since my mother and I just shared a few teary-eyed minutes together, I'm either fresh out of feelings or close to exceeding today's quota.

After striding to the center of the room, Max turns around slowly, one of his hands fussing with the collar of his button-down. That's the biggest sign that something's amiss: He isn't wearing the light gray suit Andrew selected for his attendants.

I prod him with a different question. "Is Andrew okay?"

It can't be that bad if Max is here. I don't know him well—he lives in New York and hasn't been around for most of the pre-wedding festivities. Still, he's Andrew's only sibling, and if something awful has happened, he'd be with his older brother, right? Well, given that Max was Andrew's third choice for best man (after choices one and two politely declined), perhaps that isn't a safe assumption.

Max scrunches his brows, the resulting lines in his forehead reminding me of ripples in water. "No, no, Andrew's fine. It's nothing like that."

I press a hand to my belly and let out a shaky breath. "All right, good. Then what's going on?"

He swallows. Hard. "He's not coming. To the wedding. Says he can't go through with it."

For several seconds, I just blink and process. Blink, blink, blink, and process. *God.* All the planning. The people. The family that traveled from near and far to be here. I envision the fallout and cringe. My mother and aunts will be livid on my behalf. Before this day is over, they'll organize a search party so they can find Andrew and kick him in the balls with the agility and precision of the Rockettes. And considering their entrepreneurial spirit, I wouldn't be surprised if they sold tickets to the show and titled it *The Nutcracker.*

Max clears his throat. The staccato sound disrupts my stream of consciousness, and the significance of the situation truly hits me.

I'm not getting married today.

My throat constricts and my chest tightens. *Oh, no, no, no. Hold it together, Lina. You're a pro at this.* I wrestle with my tears and body slam them back into their ducts.

Max inches forward. "What can I do? Do you need a hug? A shoulder to cry on?"

"I don't know what I need," I say hoarsely, unable to pull off the unruffled demeanor I'd hoped to convey.

His sad eyes meet mine and he opens his arms. I step into his embrace, desperate to connect with someone so I'll feel less . . . adrift. He holds me with a light touch, and somehow I know he's restraining himself, as though he wants to keep me afloat rather than pull me under. Through the fog, I notice Max is damp, fresh from a shower possibly, and I'm struck by the absence of any detectible fragrance on his skin. I wonder briefly if my scent will cling to him when he leaves, then wonder just as briefly whether my brain's short-circuiting.

"Are you okay?" he asks in a whisper-soft tone.

I don't move as I consider his question. Maybe remaining still will help me assess the damage. By all rights, I should be hurt, angry, ready to rail against the injustice of what Andrew's done to me. But I'm none of those things. Not yet. The truth is, I'm numb—and more than a little confused.

Andrew's supposed to be "the one." For two years, we've shared interesting conversations, satisfying sex, and stability. Most important, he's never pushed my buttons—not even once —and I can't imagine a better choice for a lifelong partner than someone who doesn't trigger my worst impulses. Until this morning, Andrew and I seemed to be on the same page about the mutual benefits of this union. Today he's apparently in a different book altogether—and I have no idea why.

Max fills the silence, babbling for us both: "I don't know what's going on with him. One minute he was fine. And then we talked last night. We went barhopping, you know? Somewhere between the shots of Patrón, I said some foolish things. It went sideways from there. I'm sorry. So damn sorry."

The anguish in his voice snags my attention, gives me a hook to sink my psyche into. He's apologizing for something rather than consoling me, which doesn't make sense. I slip out of his arms and back away. "What do you mean you said some foolish things?"

He drops his chin and stares at the floor. "Honestly, I don't remember all that much. I was drunk."

I skirt around him so I'm not blinded by the sunlight streaming in from the arched bay window—the better to see this fuckery. Oh, the cloudless sky chafes, too; wasting perfect wedding-day weather should be a petty crime punishable by at least a few days' jail time. "How'd he tell you? Did you speak to him face-to-face?"

"He sent a text," Max says softly, the floor still the object of his undivided attention.

"Let me see it," I demand.

His head shoots up at the command. For a few seconds, we do nothing but stare at each other. He flares his nostrils. I . . . don't. His gaze darts to my lips, which part of their own volition—until I realize what I'm doing and snap my mouth shut.

My body temperature rises, and I'm tempted to tug at the lace on my arms and chest. I feel itchy all over, as if millions of fire ants are marching across my skin to the tune of Beyoncé's "Formation." I mentally push away the discomfort and hold out my hand. "I need to see what he wrote." When he doesn't budge, I add, "Please."

Max blows out a long breath, then reaches into the back

pocket of his jeans, pulls out his phone, and taps on the screen. "Here."

With my lips pursed in concentration, I read the jumble of sentences confirming that I, Lina Santos, a twenty-five-year-old up-and-coming wedding planner to DC professionals, am officially a jilted bride. *Wow. Okay. Just. Yeah.* I couldn't be more off-brand if I tried.

Still studying Andrew's text, I narrow my eyes on the sentence that annoys me the most: *Thanks to you, I can see the truth now.*

Oh, really? And what truth did you help my fiancé see, Max? Hmm? God, I can just imagine those two talking crap about me in some grimy pub. Makes me want to scream.

I shove the phone back into his hand. "So to sum up: You and Andrew got shit-faced last night, chatted about something you claim not to remember, based on that conversation he's decided not to marry me, and he doesn't have the decency to tell me any of this himself."

Max is slow to agree, but eventually he nods. "That's the sense I get, yes."

"He's a dick," I say flatly.

"I won't argue with that," Max replies, the beginnings of a smile daring to appear at the corners of his trash-talking mouth.

"And you're an asshole."

His face sours, but I refuse to give a rat's ass about his feelings. Whatever nonsense he spouted off last night convinced my fiancé to tank our wedding. I'd been *so close* to marrying the right man for me, and a single drunken conversation derailed everything.

I straighten and grab my own phone off the dressing table, sending out an SOS to my mother, aunts, and cousins:

Me: Eu preciso de vocês agora.

93

Telling them I need them now will get their attention; doing so in Portuguese will get them here within seconds. In the meantime, I scowl at the worst best man I could have ever asked for. "Max, do me a favor, will you?"

He takes a step in my direction, his eyes pleading for forgiveness. "Anything."

"Get. The fuck. Out."

———

Want more? Order The Worst Best Man from your retailer of choice today!

ALSO BY MIA SOSA

The Starter Ex (coming soon)

The Worst Best Man
The Wedding Crasher

Acting on Impulse
Pretending He's Mine
Crashing Into Her

Unbuttoning the CEO
One Night with the CEO
Getting Dirty with the CEO

Amor Actually: A Holiday Romance Anthology

ABOUT THE AUTHOR

USA Today bestselling and award-winning author Mia Sosa writes funny, flirty, and moderately steamy contemporary romances that celebrate our multicultural world.

Booklist called her "the new go-to author for fans of sassy and sexy contemporary romances," and Cosmopolitan said Mia is "a master of the modern romance novel." Her trade paperback debut, The Worst Best Man, was awarded a Ripped Bodice Award for Excellence in Romantic Fiction, won first place in the romance category of the International Latino Book Awards, received starred reviews from Kirkus, Publishers Weekly, and Booklist, and was named one of the best romances of 2020 by Entertainment Weekly, NPR, Oprah Magazine, Buzzfeed, Insider, Cosmopolitan, Kobo, and more. Her latest release, *The Wedding Crasher*, received starred reviews from Publishers Weekly, Booklist, Library Journal, and BookPage and was a Best Romance nominee in the 2022 Goodreads Choice Awards. In its starred review, Publishers Weekly described The Wedding Crasher as a "brilliant follow-up to The Worst Best Man."

Before starting a writing career, Mia practiced First Amendment and media law in the nation's capital. Now she spends her days plotting stories and procrastinating on social media. Born and raised in East Harlem, New York, Mia is finally ready to call Maryland her home; she lives there with her husband, their two daughters, and a couple of pets that rule them all.

To learn more about Mia and her work, visit miasosa.com.

Made in United States
North Haven, CT
03 August 2023

39903493R00067